EDGE OF THE GALAXY

30 FAITH-FILLED ADVENTURES

BROCK EASTMAN

FOCUS ON THE FAMILY.

A Focus on the Family Resource
Published by Tyndale House Publishers

To Kinley, Elise, Waverly, Declan,

*This book is for you. Your generation will be the first to live in colonies
on the Moon and on Mars, the first to step foot on Titan and Europa.
Your generation will change not only the world but also the galaxy.*

*I pray God does great things with your lives, that He blesses you abundantly,
and that you would each serve Him wholeheartedly and unapologetically.*

I love each of you to the edge of the galaxy and beyond!

Edge of the Galaxy: 30 Faith-Filled Adventures
© 2023 Brock Eastman. All rights reserved.

Cover and interior illustrations by Rahmat Saleh Pasa. Copyright © 2023 by Crimson Pulse Media. All rights reserved.

A Focus on the Family book published by Tyndale House Publishers, Carol Stream, Illinois 60188

Focus on the Family and its accompanying logos and designs are federally registered trademarks of Focus on the Family, 8605 Explorer Drive, Colorado Springs, CO 80920.

Tyndale and Tyndale's quill logo are registered trademarks of Tyndale House Ministries.

All Scripture quotations, unless otherwise marked, are from The Holy Bible, English Standard Version. Copyright © 2001 by CrosswayBibles, a publishing ministry of Good News Publishers. Used by permission. All rights reserved.

Scripture quotations marked (NIV) are taken from the Holy Bible, New International Version,® NIV.® Copyright © 1973, 1978, 1984 by Biblica, Inc.® Used by permission of Zondervan. All rights reserved worldwide. (www.zondervan.com) The "NIV" and "New International Version" are trademarks registered in the United States Patent and Trademark Office by Biblica, Inc.®

For Library of Congress Cataloging-in-Publication Data for this title, visit http://www.loc.gov/help/contact-general.html.

For manufacturing information regarding this product, please call 1-855-277-9400.

For information about special discounts for bulk purchases, please contact Tyndale House Publishers at csresponse@tyndale.com, or call 1-855-277-9400.

Printed in China

ISBN 978-1-64607-067-1

29	28	27	26	25	24	23
7	6	5	4	3	2	1

Welcome to Titan!

Greetings! I am KEWD, the Artificial Intelligence (AI) system for the Greystone family. The information in this guide will help you understand more about the planet Saturn and its moon Titan on which you will adventure.

The sixth planet from the sun, Saturn is very far outside the Earth's orbit. It takes Saturn twenty-nine Earth years to complete its path around the sun! That means a "season" on Saturn is about seven years long.

Saturn is huge—the second-largest planet in our solar system after Jupiter. You could fit over 760 Earth-sized planets inside Saturn. But as a gas giant, the planet doesn't have a surface—it's made mostly of hot gases and liquids. Any spacecraft that tries to land on or fly through Saturn would be destroyed by the high temperatures and pressure within the planet.

Titan is the largest of Saturn's moons and the second-largest known moon in our solar system. Titan is tidally locked to Saturn just as Earth's moon—we call it Luna—is tidally locked to Earth. This means that Titan takes the same amount of time to rotate around its own axis as it does to revolve around Saturn. So the same side of Titan is always pointed toward Saturn, just as people on Earth always see the same side of the moon, wherever they are on the planet.

Titan's surface is formed of mostly rock-hard ice—extremely frozen water. The surface also has lakes and rivers made of liquid methane because this moon is exceptionally frigid. The average temperature is -289 degrees Fahrenheit, or -178.889 Celsius.

Below Titan's surface is an ocean of water that is highly salty; this liquid is composed of hydrogen and oxygen, much like the oceans on Earth.

The Alliance of Spacefaring Nations (ASN) began exploring Titan with remote probes over twenty years ago. The alliance gathered scientists and engineers to figure out how humanity could one day live on that moon. Now that an ASN flag has been planted on Titan, the Greystones are fulfilling the alliance's vision of establishing the first human settlement on Saturn's frigid moon.

Greetings from the orbital platform *Provider*!

My name is Gavin Greystone, and I live here on *Provider* with my family. My dad's name is Phoenix, my mom is Nebula, my brother is Comet, and my sister is Aurora. You could say my family is living on the edge—both because we're living on the furthest edge of human civilization, and because our work out here is so dangerous.

Here on *Provider*, we are somewhere between 746 million and one billion miles from Earth, depending on our current position in the solar system. That's a long way from our home planet! *Provider* orbits Titan, one of Saturn's moons, and it was built by the Alliance of Spacefaring Nations (ASN).

Five years ago, my family arrived at *Provider* on board a space-ship called *Beyond*. I was seven years old at the time. We moved here from Mars to oversee the construction of Inspire, the first human settlement on Titan and soon to be our new home.

We have an artificial intelligence system named KEWD. (Don't ask me what it stands for because no one ever told me.) This AI is built into all of our computer systems, helping us with our work and with living life out here in space. Most of our work on the surface of Titan is done remotely by our team of constructo-bots. With KEWD's help, my family creates these robots' tasks, verifies their work, and solves problems that happen along the way.

There are a few other people aboard *Provider* too. Their job is making sure the station continues to function, communicating with the ASN command center on Earth, and conducting other experiments. But when it comes to establishing a settlement on Titan, it's the Greystone family or bust. We are a hundred percent on the hook for the success or failure of our habitat, called a hab-dome, on Titan's surface. Eventually, the Inspire settlement will include other hab-domes, but completing this one is our first priority.

Our family has trained hard to become a fantastic team. Not that we don't have the occasional setback or argument! My brother, Comet, likes to be in charge (even though he isn't), and my sister, Aurora, thinks she has the answer to every problem (even though she doesn't). I don't let either of them push me around. I may be the youngest, but I'm taller than both of them, and I read a lot because, well, there isn't a lot else to do out here at what feels like the edge of the galaxy.

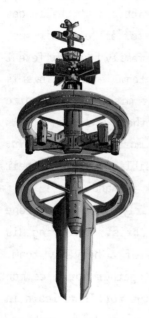

Dad and Mom are good about keeping us focused on our mission and helping us work out our differences. They take time to help each of us develop our own skill sets even if, at times, these skills aren't necessarily something we want to learn. For example, why do I have to know how to solve math problems when KEWD can do all the calculations for me through my mTalk? I mean, isn't that why we all have mTalk devices—to communicate, access information, and help us solve problems?

If all goes according to plan, Team Greystone will be departing from *Provider* to the surface of Titan next week to become the first settlers there, making us the third group to establish a settlement on a moon or planet beyond Earth (after the colonies on Luna and Mars). We'll be the very first humans to touch the surface of Titan! That's mind-blowing to think about. I'll be walking in places where no human has ever been. *Amazing!*

Our current team consists of my family members, but it'll soon expand with two additional families joining us down on Titan. And from there, our settlement will continue to grow. For now though, my parents will lead our family and the two additional families coming to Titan. I hope someday I'll be as good at leading a team as they are.

IIIIIIIIFaiTH aT THe eDGe: Teamwork

Hello, this is KEWD again. I'll be extracting insights from Gavin's daily journal entry to take you deeper into some of the challenges he is facing.

The Greystone family is a team. No matter what challenges come their way, they rely on each other for all of their successes and failures. Each person in their family has a different skill set that makes them all valuable team members. This is important to help them succeed in their mission to colonize Titan. No role is more important than another; each position is unique and helps the team work together more effectively. Mr. and Mrs. Greystone help Gavin and his siblings sharpen their skills and keep them focused on the task at hand.

The Christian life works very similarly to the Greystone team. When you put your trust in Jesus Christ, accepting His offer of salvation, you become a part of a heavenly team. This is a team of Christians working together for a common goal or task: to share God's love with the world! We learn in 1 Corinthians 12 that this team is similar to the human body. Each part of the body has an essential job, and one part cannot work as effectively without the other. The Bible says that God put each part exactly where He wanted it.

> God arranged the members in the body, each one of them, as he chose. If all were a single member, where would the body be? As it is, there are many parts, yet one body.
> —1 CORINTHIANS 12:18-20

Just like Gavin's parents help him and his siblings stay focused and sharpen their skills, the Lord does the same for you. He puts people in your life to help you grow in your relationship with Him, and He'll develop your skills so that you can work effectively with your Christian team.

Gavin's family is part of a critical team working together to achieve the goal of establishing a settlement on Titan. You, as a Christian, are also a part of an essential spiritual team working together to achieve the purpose of sharing Jesus with the world. So remember that God loves you and values you as part of His fantastic team.

EXPLORATION ------------------------

1. What teams have you been a part of? What role did you play on those teams?

2. Did you feel that your strengths were used in these roles? Or is there something else you would have liked to try?

3. Read 1 Corinthians 12. What is the reason we are a team? How has being part of a team strengthened you? How has being part of a team helped you realize the value of having people with different gifts and skills?

With only eight days until we land on Titan, our list of tasks seems almost insurmountable. This morning my mom needed my assistance on a booster refit for our Titan lander, which meant we had to do a spacewalk.

I know space "walking" isn't a normal thing for most twelve-year-olds, but it's what I was born for—or at least it feels like I was born for it. My parents began training me on the techniques, nuances, and dangers of spacewalking as soon as I could wear a walker-suit (our nickname for ASN's ExoSuits that we wear in space). I learned to spacewalk about a year after we got to *Provider*.

My brother and sister each have their strengths, but neither are as adept at spacewalking as I am. Comet wouldn't admit this, but he's really not very good in a walker-suit, and he usually only takes on things he knows he can do well. So, when there is a repair needed on a constructo-bot or on *Hopper*, which is our Titan lander, I'm the one my parents ask.

Today's spacewalk was pretty easy, nothing extreme. We didn't have to travel too far from the airlock hatch. We've trained and trained, and we always go in pairs, which is usually my mom and me. For me, this is part of my routine. As we begin the final week before we depart for Titan, I've been spacewalking nearly every day.

The truth is, when I'm on the outside of the orbital station, I feel free. Knowing there are millions of miles of empty black space around me is mind-blowing. That vast emptiness will be what I will miss most once my family is moon-bound on Titan.

Our task today shouldn't have been difficult, but we ran into a complication. A system check on *Hopper* had registered an error code in the lander's booster number two. After a diagnostic scan, KEWD identified the issue as a malfunction with the booster's fuel pod. The whole pod had to be replaced.

I knew exactly how to do the repair thanks to KEWD over-laying my Heads-Up Display (HUD) with instructions on the inside of my helmet. KEWD even highlighted the parts that needed to be fixed. While my mom did a visual check on the booster cone itself, I retrieved my Magnilox tool from my satchel. I began to loosen the discharge line for the booster.

Suddenly, the line burst from its connector and slammed into my chest, flinging me backward. My body crashed against one of the station's many solar panels. I felt my walker-suit snag on something sharp, and instantly my helmet's integrated display lit up with a warning. KEWD read the words aloud in a calm, serious

tone: "ExoSuit compromised. Counter pressurization activated. Proceed to airlock immediately. Sixty seconds until pressurization failure."

Sixty seconds? Must be a big rip.

My tether was looped through several safety hooks along the way to the airlock. There was no way for me to make my way back to the airlock in sixty seconds. But if I disconnected my tether, I could make it before I lost all my air.

I reached for the connection between the tether and my ExoSuit.

"Gavin, stop," my mom said, her voice calm.

"No, I have to get to the airlock. I can't get there in time if I am hooked to the tether."

"Gavin, you have to remain calm. Trust your training."

"Forty-five seconds," KEWD interjected.

I couldn't see her. She was on the underside of the lander. "Mom, I only have forty-five seconds," my voice quivered. I was starting to freak out.

"Stay calm," she said. "You can do this."

I had trained for emergencies. I had practiced remaining calm, or at least trying to compose myself before taking action. So I took a deep breath, then closed my eyes.

"You have an emergency seal tube in your right sleeve pocket," she said.

I unzipped the pocket, and the tube floated free. I took it and popped the cap loose. Thick white goo began to slither out.

"Thirty seconds," KEWD said. "Proceed to airlock immediately."

"I can't see the rip."

"Trust me, son," my mom said. "Reach directly behind your

head, then lower your hand until your fingers reach the spot between your shoulder blades." The calmness in her voice gave me peace too.

I followed her directions. "Am I there?"

"Twenty seconds. Proceed to airlock immediately." KEWD's calm tone seemed to have more urgency to it now.

"Yes, and I am here too," she said. And there she was. She had reached me! She took the tube and squeezed a liquid patch across the hole at the back of my walker-suit.

"Pressure stabilized," KEWD said calmly once again. "Proceed to airlock immediately."

What a relief! With the hole patched, we had more time to get back to the airlock. Once we'd gotten safely back inside *Provider* and removed our walker-suits, I hugged my mom tightly. "Thank you, Mom. I was so scared."

"Gavin, you know I'll always be there to help."

"I know. How'd you remain so calm?"

"Well, it wasn't easy for me, either. I relied on my training, and I trusted God," she said. "And He delivered."

IIIIIIFAITH AT THE EDGE: TRUST

Gavin is confident in his abilities. He has been extensively trained for spacewalking, and the skill comes naturally to him. However, the minute something went wrong, it became difficult for him to trust in his training, and fear took over.

Training might equip Gavin with the knowledge to handle various challenges, but training alone wasn't enough to give him what he needed to survive. He couldn't stay calm or decide what to do until his mom reminded him to trust in his training.

She knew how to rely on their training and how to ultimately trust in God. But how was that possible?

Gavin's mom trusted in the Lord because she had learned about who He was and how He could help her through life. That was a big part of her training.

As a Christian, do you recognize how your training prepares you for life's challenges? Your training begins at the moment of salvation when you accept Jesus Christ as your Savior, allowing Him to guide your life. Then, by reading your Bible and joining a church, you learn about who He is and how He helps you make decisions. Through Christian community, you learn more about God's love and truth. As you gain a deeper understanding of the Lord, you grow in your relationship with Him, learning to trust in His loving design.

> It is the LORD who goes before you. He will be with you; he will not leave you or forsake you. Do not fear or be dismayed.
> —DEUTERONOMY 31:8

You can trust that the Lord will go before you. He knows what is going to happen, and He also promises that He will never leave you. He walks with you as you experience troubled times. You do not have to be afraid because you can trust in Him. When you remember who He is and how He can help, fear will not take over in moments of trouble.

Gavin's mom remained calm because she knew that God was going before them and walking with them. When she put her trust in the Lord, her training did not fail her. When you put your trust in the Lord, your training—what you have learned about the Lord—will help you in every situation just like it did for Gavin and his mom.

EXPLORATION -----------------------

1. Write about a time when you put your trust in God. Looking back, do you see where and how God was in that situation?

2. Read Deuteronomy 31:1-8. What do you think it means that the Lord "goes before you?" How can you better recognize the evidence that He is indeed in front of you?

3. What are some ways you can learn and grow to trust God more?

With two new families—seven additional people in total—arriving on *Provider* in the next week, there was a lot of other work to be done in addition to the tasks required for my family's mission to Titan. My sister, Aurora, and I were assigned to set up one of the two empty living pods. The pods in this section of the orbital station still had to be furnished with beds, storage, a sitting area, and a workstation. And since *Provider* has simulated gravity, the task wouldn't be as easy as zero-g pie.

It wasn't that I didn't know what to do—KEWD had loaded the diagram for the new spaces on my mTab and the materials to complete the task were just outside in the corridor. I was confident I could handle this job; I'm good at working with my hands, at construction, and at general problem-solving. The problem was . . . *why*. I wasn't going to be living in this pod. My family was already doing all the work preparing the settlement on Titan.

Why couldn't the newcomers build their own pods?

"All right, no more procrastinating," Aurora said. "We've got to get this done. We need to start with the beds. Since this one is for the Evolt family, we only need three."

I took a deep breath and tapped the mTab. "What kind of name is Evolt?"

"What kind of name is Gavin?" Aurora countered, retrieving a long pole from the corridor.

"I still don't understand why we have to do this," I said. "It's not written in our mission requirements to set up other families' beds. We had to set up our own."

But Aurora was focused. She locked a long support pole into place and then disappeared into the corridor for another. I followed and grabbed the netted bed frame. Once the second support was in place, I attached the bunk.

"We don't even know these people," I said. "I mean, not really. Sure, we've had vid-chats, but we don't really know them. And Comet said they aren't our type of people."

Aurora stopping working for a moment and sighed. But then we got back on task. Once all three bunks were set up, the sitting area was next. We deployed a wide foam couch along with two chairs. Then we constructed a low, round table, using materials from out in the corridor. I grunted and plopped onto the couch, sinking into the responsive foam. "I think we've done enough."

Aurora turned and lowered herself into a chair, then folded her hands. "Gavin, you've been complaining about this job a lot," she began. "Do you recall the oath you took?"

My cheeks warmed.

"To serve others by selflessly going beyond the known limits of humankind," Aurora quoted. "Did you know this was meant to speak not only to geographical or physical limits but also to our mental and emotional limits?"

Sure, I knew that. My parents had explained it to me, using a story from the Bible. I knew Aurora was about to remind me of that.

"Comet's right in the fact that we are different from those who will be joining us on Titan, but our difference is exactly why we are setting up this pod. And remember that we are not only called to serve others, but to do so selflessly and often without reward," Aurora said. "It's like the story of Jesus washing the feet of His disciples. The disciples considered Him their master, yet He served them by washing their dirty feet. He wasn't required to; He did it to selflessly serve them, to show them compassion and love."

"I . . ." Words escaped me; I knew she was right. But sometimes it was hard to live out what I read in the Bible, to be what I proclaimed to be.

"Look, Gav, I know it's not easy. We've been working hard for a long time to prepare for this moment, and it feels like these two families are coming after we've put so much into this—and they will get to benefit from all our hard work." Aurora paused and leaned forward. "But that's also what we get to do. We get to benefit from what Jesus did on the cross. So what really matters is that by our servanthood, others might come to know the love of Jesus. As Christians, we're called to a higher standard."

I nodded, "You're right. I'm sorry for complaining."

"No one said any of this would be easy," she said. "Whether exploring a celestial body in space or serving the Creator of it all, we'll always face challenges and adversity. Compared to some of the trials that other Christians throughout history have faced, this is pretty easy. But it might not always be, so we need to prepare however we can."

"Yeah, I guess I can finish a few more pieces of furniture," I said. I stood and pulled Aurora to her feet. "I'll try to do it with a smile on my face—and in my heart."

"That's the way," Aurora said.

|||||FAITH AT THE EDGE: SERVANT'S HEART

Sometimes it's a challenge to help others out, and it can be even more difficult to help while having a good attitude and not complaining.

Aurora reminded Gavin about the time Jesus washed the feet of His disciples. Back in Jesus' time, men and women walked everywhere in sandals. The roads were made of dirt, which meant there was a lot of mud when it rained. On top of that, the primary means of transportation were horses, donkeys, and camels. Now what do you think was left all over the roads?

All that to say, feet are pretty gross. Yet without hesitation, Jesus filled a bowl with water, knelt before His disciples, and washed their feet. Jesus wanted them to follow His example and show others the same kind of compassion and love He showed them.

Leaders aren't more important than those who follow. And those who follow aren't more important than those who lead. God created every single person. He wants His children to be an example of His love to everyone they encounter.

EXPLORATION --------------------

1. Read the story of Jesus washing the feet of His disciples found in John 13:1-20. What can you learn about the heart of Jesus from the way He treats His disciples?

2. How can you be an example of God's love for the people you know? How can you be an example of God's love to a stranger?

More work! And it's a day of meaningless work—inventory. This was not fun, this is not what I'm good at, this will be boring!

I tapped my mTab and then spoke, "Twelve."

KEWD responded through my mTab, "Twelve expected; inventory confirmed."

The number "12" appeared next to "Graviton cylinders." I opened another compartment and began counting. I tapped the mTab. "Forty-seven," I said. KEWD confirmed that this was the expected number, and "47" appeared next to "Graviton secure bolts."

"Uhhhh!" I groaned, growing more bored by the minute. The hatch was shut, so no one could hear my misery.

"Finish today, or come back and finish tomorrow. Or the day after that—and so on," my dad had warned. There was no avoiding this task. My dad is the Titan Mission Commander, and I'm his subordinate.

Feeling like a soldier more than a son, I marched over to the next supply pod and opened the first drawer. The sight of Energen drinks brought a smile to my face. The fizzy, vitamin-enhanced Energen drinks are my absolute favorite. But I'm allowed one only on rare occasions due to limited supply. (Still, I've often wondered: Since Energen drinks have so many vitamins, shouldn't I be consuming them more often?)

I counted the cans. There were only two dozen left. I tapped the mTab. "Twenty-four."

"Incorrect inventory," KEWD said. "Please recount."

"Ugh." I counted again and still came up with twenty-four. "Twenty-four," I repeated loudly.

"Incorrect inventory. Request supervisor override to update inventory," KEWD said.

And then I saw that my mTab showed there should only be twelve cans of Energen. The other dozen weren't in the system. Why not smuggle the extra twelve cans back to my pod and slip them into my compartment? Then I could have one on occasion when I chose. No one would ever know.

I tapped the mTab again. "Twelve." The AI confirmed the expected quantity and noted it next to the right entry. I picked up the extra twelve cans.

Then the hatch opened. "Hey, Gav," my mom said. "How's it going?"

Quickly turning so that my mom couldn't see what I was

holding, I set the cans against the wall of the supply pod and covered them with a sack used for transporting goods.

In a robotic voice, I groaned, "Slow and boring. And more boring."

As my mom came into the pod, an odd feeling swept over me. I could feel the presence of the cans over there by the wall. I glanced at them. I tried to stop myself, but I felt an almost magnetic force drawing my attention back.

Mom smiled. "I know, Gav, but even though this task is monotonous, it's critical. We only get three supply shipments a year, and *Beyond* doesn't have extra cargo space. We must order the right quantity, and we can only do that with an accurate inventory list."

"Yes, Mom, I know."

She clicked her tongue. "Well, did you need an override for something?"

The back of my neck prickled as every hair stood on end, and my stomach did a tiny somersault. "Huh?"

"KEWD sent an alert to my mTalk requesting an inventory quantity override," she said.

I'd forgotten about KEWD's automatic alerts. What was I going to do? If I tell her I did need the override, she'd look in the compartment and see only twelve Energen cans since the *extra* twelve Energen were near the door, under the sack. If I said "no," I'd be lying. The guilt was swirling in me like a Martian tornado, which I've heard are huge compared to Earth's tornadoes. I knew I should have never removed the cans.

Technically I hadn't stolen the Energen drinks yet; they were still in the pod. I could just tell Mom, "no," then return the cans, and no one would be any wiser, and my guilt would vanish.

"No," I said quickly. "I . . . I miscounted."

"It happens," she said. "You're dealing with a lot of numbers." She started back for the hatch and stopped. "I know this job is tedious, but it is essential. Your father and I trust you."

The guilt tornado ramped up again, spinning faster and faster.

"Thanks, Mom," I said. "I won't let you down."

When she was gone, I grabbed the extra Energen cans and placed them back in the drawer. I tapped the mTab, found the listing, and updated the quantity.

"Error, supervisor approval required," KEWD said again.

I thumped my forehead. I knew then I would have to own up to the lie.

A moment later, the hatch opened. My mom stepped in. "KEWD must be acting up," she began. "I got another alert for an override."

I shook my head. "Mom, I need to tell you something."

"What's that, Gavin?" my mom asked.

"Well, you see . . ." I began. There were a lot of emotions swirling inside me at that moment. Confessing—trying to overcome my guilt and my fear of getting in trouble and disappointing my parents—was hard. But I knew what I had to do, and I knew the best thing I could do would be to come clean, and the sooner I did it, the better.

"Mom, there are actually twenty-four cans of Energen in the drawer," I said. "I gave in to temptation when KEWD said there were only twelve cans. I was going to take the extra twelve cans for myself."

In that instant, the guilt tornado was gone; all the dirt swirling inside me blew away, and I could see clearly and breathe easily again.

My mom nodded. "I see. Thank you for telling the truth. Thank you for being honest not only with the inventory, but with sharing your intentions and actions."

She looked over the inventory, tapped her mTab, and said, "Override confirmed. Twenty-Four."

My mom passed her hand through my hair, ruffling as she did. "Alright, Gav, back to work."

"But aren't I in trouble?"

"No, you're not," my mom said.

I probably looked like a fish, with my mouth open so wide.

"You told the truth. It's possible that you would have gotten away with the lie, or you may have been caught. But the truth and the lie would have been yours, inside you. Eventually, the guilt would have become a burden too heavy to carry around. The truth would have come out."

She took a deep breath and looked directly into my eyes. "Gav, you've professed to be a Christian, so God's Holy Spirit works within you; that is why you confessed to me. And God is doing a new work within you. Within all of us. We're human, and we still sin, but we are striving to be as Christlike as we can while in this realm."

I knew by "this realm," she meant "this world." In the past, people had said, "while we are on this Earth," but we are galactic explorers who no longer live on Earth, so we began using the term, "realm."

"Okay, Mom, thanks," I said. And with that, she turned to leave. I expected her to tell my dad. After all, they had no secrets between each other, but I was certain I'd never hear of the incident again. I'd done the right thing, and she'd forgiven me.

|||||||||||FAITH AT THE EDGE: HONESTY

Gavin lied and was tempted to steal. He might have been able to hide his sin from everyone else, but both he and God would still have known what he did. Gavin couldn't escape his feelings of guilt and the need to confess.

King David described similar feelings in Psalm 51 after he had sinned. Knowing that only God could take away his guilt, David confessed and acknowledged God's right to judge him.

Likewise, Gavin knew he deserved punishment, but his mom decided to mercifully withhold that punishment since he voluntarily came to her and confessed.

> Create in me a clean heart, O God, and renew a right spirit within me. Cast me not away from your presence, and take not your Holy Spirit from me. Restore to me the joy of your salvation, and uphold me with a willing spirit.
>
> —PSALM 51:10-12

Everyone can get trapped by the temptation to sin. But Paul encourages Christians in 1 Corinthians 10:13 that God will always help them escape. Jesus promises His disciples that the Holy Spirit, "the Spirit of truth," will always be with them to help them (John 14:15-18, 26). Paul further admonishes believers to "not grieve the Holy Spirit of God" by continuing to live in sin but to let God change their lives to look more like Jesus (Ephesians 4:17-32).

Still, mistakes happen. Take comfort in these words: "If we confess our sins, he is faithful and just to forgive

us our sins and to cleanse us from all unrighteousness"
(1 John 1:9).

EXPLORATION ------------------------

1. Recall a recent time when have you been tempted to sin.
    How did you respond to that temptation?

2. Is there anything you need to confess? Is there a sin that
    seems particularly tempting to you?

3. Can the Holy Spirit help you avoid giving in to temptation?
    Write down some practical ideas that can help you be more
    sensitive to the Spirit's guidance during situations where
    you are tempted to sin.

K EWD hadn't even sent its typical robotic "Good morning, this is your wake-up call" message to my mTalk, blasting annoying music over the speakers, before I bolted upright and threw off my covers.

Today's the day!

My brother, Comet, had promised I could watch him activate the new methane extraction compressors that would be used to extract methane from Titan's atmosphere and then compress it for storage so it could be used as rocket fuel. I had tried to get Comet to let me activate the extractors, but he insisted on doing it himself. He said I didn't have the training he did and that I'd probably mess something up. Personally, I think he just didn't want to turn over the best part of the project to his "little" brother, who happens to be taller than him.

I tried to persuade Mom and Dad to train me on the extraction process and equipment, but they chose Comet. I thought it would be so cool to make rocket fuel. But I had already been assigned spacewalking as my primary training.

This morning, I was excited to get started. I splashed a bit of water on my face and hustled down the corridors to the command module.

I thrust open the doors to find the Titan Operations Command Module empty. *Where was Comet?* There was no one in the command module.

The vid-screens on the wall give live feeds from Inspire. The largest screen in the center showed that the two methane extraction compressors were offline and that the two constructo-bots (CB-83 and CB-85) were on standby. Several other vid-screens showed other constructo-bots actively working on their assignments: cleaning dust from solar arrays, collecting ice samples from a nearby cryovolcano, clearing and flattening an area for the next hab-dome to be constructed.

Humph! He can't even show up on time to finish this critical assignment. One more reason I should have been the one to train with the extractors.

I waited and waited. And then waited some more. At least ten minutes had passed. I glanced at my mTalk on my wrist. Well, okay, only five minutes had passed. *Still, where was Comet?*

I couldn't stand it any longer. What is the old saying from Earth, "You snooze, you lose"?

If Comet wasn't going to be responsible enough to be here on time, then he didn't deserve to have this job. I hopped into Comet's

seat at the console. Swiping my fingers across the various screens and buttons, I discovered that Comet had already programmed the robots to make the final connection to activate the extractors and then begin extracting methane from the atmosphere.

I tapped the icon to make the operation active. The robots came out of standby mode. The extractors remained offline. The constructo-bots' arms came to life, shifting into position. Each arm had a different implement to conduct the operation.

"KEWD, initiate activation for methane extraction compressor, unit one," I said.

Two icons appeared on the vid-screen, one for "activate" and one for "stand down," along with the question, "Activate methane extraction compressor, unit 1?" overhead.

My fingers touched:

"Activate"

The constructo-bots began to operate. Sparks flew as one bot used a welder torch to fuse an exhaust pipe to the outside of the extractor. The second robot began plugging power connectors to a wide panel at the base of the extractor. Everything was going precisely as it was supposed to.

Suddenly a jet of gas erupted from a pipe joint that fed into the extractor compression chamber! *Yikes! Some kind of leak?* An alert appeared on the screen on the console, and KEWD spoke: "Methane extraction compressor online. Gas stabilization inactive. Rapid pressure increase detected."

I leaned forward, searching the interactive screen before me and wondering what command to give the constructo-bot.

An alarm in the Titan Operations Command Module blared to life.

KEWD spoke again, with urgency: "Explosion imminent. Please cease methane extraction. Manual shutdown required."

"Oh, what did I do? God, please help me!" I cried out, searching for a setting I could adjust that might help.

On the main vid-screen, I could see dust billowing from where methane gas was shooting back out of the compressor, where the pipe was still unattached. What could I do? I kept looking under menu screens and tapping on the alerts.

I wondered if the extractor was filling up with methane gas. Was it going to explode? Sweat poured down my face as another alert from KEWD rang out: "Estimated time to maximum pressure: three minutes. Extractor explosion imminent."

I threw my hands up in despair. An explosion of methane gas could destroy a portion of the settlement. In fact, it might even force us to find a new location for the settlement. I'd be sent back to Mars for sure.

I had to . . .

Suddenly the hatch to the command module slid open! Dad and Comet sprinted in. Comet shoved me out of the chair as he reached the console.

I'd never been so glad in my life to let him take control.

He began furiously swiping across the console screen icons. Dad took his seat at the Commander's station.

"Comet, start the emergency deactivation process," my dad ordered. "I'll move CB-83 to vent excess methane gas and then use CB-85 to realign atmospheric filtering."

"Starting emergency deactivation process," Comet responded, not even a second later.

But we weren't in the clear yet. The pressure gauge continued to increase slowly, then it stopped. Long seconds passed.

"CB-83 venting complete; CB-85 realignment complete," my dad said.

Then Comet let out a loud whoop and collapsed back into his chair. "Clear! Dad, we got it to shut off," he said between heavy breaths.

The clouds of dust slowed to a few puffs. Finally, they stopped. The extractor stopped shaking. It felt like an eternity before anyone spoke.

Comet glared at me; I still sat on the floor where I'd landed after being shoved (deservedly) from the seat at the console. I had remained stunned and unable to move, caught up in the swift movements of my dad and brother.

Finally, Dad asked, "Gavin, what happened?"

I couldn't meet his eyes as I mumbled, "I tried to activate the extractors."

"Why were you doing Comet's assignment?" he asked, turning to Comet.

"Comet wasn't here, and I thought I could do it," I mumbled even more quietly.

"I wasn't here because I realized last night that something was wrong with the program. The venting process wasn't diverting enough excess methane from the compressor. I was up until 3 a.m. trying to figure out how to adjust the pressure modulation," Comet explained. "I was at a dead end. I needed to wait until this morning to talk to Dad."

"Gavin," Dad said, "I know you're always pushing the boundaries of what you can do, and in some instances, that's a good thing. That's what helps you learn and achieve new things. But some boundaries are in place to keep you and all of us safe; that's why we gave this job to Comet. He already has the skill set to complete this project, and you do not. This project was simply too dangerous to be a training exercise for you."

Then Dad gave me a look, the look that dads are known for: the stern one, where some sort of disciplinary action was coming. "We have to be able to trust you to obey, to follow orders, and to not take unnecessary risks. Do you understand, Gavin?"

"Yes, sir, I do," I said.

"Tomorrow morning, you will report to Astrobotany for cleaning and maintenance. Dr. Sue was mentioning today that she could use some extra elbow grease in the lab," my dad explained.

"Yes, sir," I said.

Elbow grease in the astrobotany lab usually meant cleaning extremely stinky sludge like plant gunk, fish waste, and organic compost from the refuse recycle lines.

"You're dismissed to your quarters until your next assignment," my dad said.

More than the punishment to clean—more than being basically grounded to my cabin for the rest of the day—it was the disappointment in my dad's eyes that hurt.

I exited the Titan Command Operations Module with a heavy heart. I had to do better, and I wanted to show my dad I could be trusted again.

⫿⫿⫿⫿⫿FAITH AT THE EDGE: BOUNDARIES

By assigning different tasks to Gavin and Comet, Gavin's parents set boundaries for their kids. They didn't do this because they wanted to keep Gavin away from something that was good for him. They were being fair, and they understood the strengths of their two sons. Gavin's parents knew that training him to spacewalk would be the best use of Gavin's skills and that working on the methane extraction compressor would be the best use of Comet's skills. It was also a loving decision; their parents knew that letting Comet deal with the extractor would be safest for everyone.

Did you know that God also gives us boundaries? In Numbers 34, Moses shares God's boundaries for the land He promised to Israel. Take a look, and while you're there, notice God's instruction below in Numbers 33:54. How did God want the land divided? He wanted the bigger tribes to get a bigger portion and the smaller tribes to get a smaller portion. God made wise and fair decisions based on what each tribe needed.

> You shall inherit the land by lot according to your clans. To a large tribe you shall give a large inheritance, and to a small tribe you shall give a small inheritance. Wherever the lot falls for anyone, that shall be his. According to the tribes of your fathers you shall inherit.
> —NUMBERS 33:54

But God didn't just give Israel geographical boundaries. He gave them relational boundaries too, in the form of the Ten Commandments. The commandments deal with how to treat God and others—how to interact with community. These boundaries, when accepted and followed, help people live and work together.

A few days ago, you read about teamwork and how 1 Corinthians 12 uses the image of the human body to describe how Christians should work together. Can you imagine what would happen if your eye decided to try to be a nose? Or if your foot chose to act like a hand? It wouldn't work very well. Just like each part of the human body is different but essential, God gives each person on earth a different but equally vital role. Gavin learned the hard way that he shouldn't try to do his brother's job and that his parents had an excellent reason for giving different assignments to each of them.

However, like Gavin's dad said, having boundaries does not necessarily mean that you shouldn't try new things. Athletes push each part of their bodies to be as strong as possible so that together, the whole body will be strong. They push their arms to lift them higher than before, and they push their legs to carry them farther and faster than before. They exercise all parts of their bodies. But there are real physical limits. Athletes can't ask their arms or legs to break the boundaries of what God designed them to do without risking serious injury.

Today, Gavin pushed the wrong boundaries. He nearly damaged his family's work on Titan, and he definitely hurt his dad's trust in him. Maybe the next time Gavin feels restricted by a boundary, he'll remember that boundaries are put in place for a reason!

EXPLORATION -

1. What boundaries have your parents, teachers, and other authorities put in place for you? Do you know why those boundaries are there? If not, can you still trust that they are there for a good reason?

2. Have you ever broken a boundary? What happened?

3. What can you exercise and make stronger without breaking a boundary? What can you do to increase your abilities in a sport, in a musical or artistic skill, or in school?

Dampness, dirt, and fish but also mango, rose, and honey. These were the smells wafting throughout Astrobotany, the largest of all the sections of *Provider*. Astrobotany is an aquaponics greenhouse, a fully sustainable and productive farm that would provide food for our settlement down on the surface of Titan and also help start the settlement's very own greenhouse. Eventually, perhaps a century from now, the first plant life to be grown on the surface of Titan outside of a protective dome will come from plants whose ancestors grew in this lab.

A fish swam in circles as I watched; it fed on the roots of a giant lily, whose blooming flower provided pollen for bees. The bees pollinated other plants and flowers throughout the greenhouse.

The aquaponics greenhouse pod is unlike any other section of the orbital station. It's twenty times larger than any other pod, and it's essentially a "wild" environment, which means it's not controlled by KEWD's systems like the rest of the station is. The animals and insects here mostly roam free, and many of the plants have outgrown their containers and now climb and twist throughout the rafters and shelves.

Provider's Astrobotanist, Dr. Sue, takes care of the plants and animals in the pod, almost as if they were her children. Matching this love is a challenge for me; she has precise instructions for how to care for the plants in a methodical and (in my opinion) overly tedious way.

At the moment, I was using a long scrubber brush to clean the inside of the largest aquaponics tank. This tank holds more than one hundred fish, and it currently needs cleaning three times a week.

"Gavin, no, you must scrub in vertical strokes, or the grime will not come free. The tank has vertical channels molded into its walls," Dr. Sue said from nearby. She was caring for the hundred fish that had been removed from the tank and temporarily rehomed in any water-holding vessel she could get her hands on.

"Yes, ma'am," I said.

"And Gavin, we must be speedy; every moment these fish are in these temporary homes, we risk them dying, and it would take months to receive replacements," Dr. Sue said.

"Yes, ma'am," I repeated. I worked harder, making sure I was scrubbing with vertical strokes. Up and down, up and down.

KEWD not-so-helpfully spoke up from the mTalk on my wrist:

"Considering your current velocity and the square footage of the tank, it will take 37 minutes and 43 seconds to complete this task."

I groaned inwardly. Recent fungi had attacked 30 percent of the water plants, and now there was an imbalance in the tank. Dr. Sue was working to bring balance back through what she called the "critical scientific methodology." She is always explaining how the scientific process can be used to solve problems.

Yes, I made a mistake. I nearly caused an uncontrolled methane explosion on Titan's surface. But, as I scrubbed that filthy tank, the punishment seemed more extreme than what the crime required. The task was smelly, grimy, dirty. And stinky. I was able to find a mask and nose plugs, but I'll probably be showering three times a day for a week just to get rid of the smell.

Suddenly a bird swooped down. Well, it didn't really swoop . . . more like it tumbled through the air. Even with artificial gravity, the birds sometimes still have a tough time flying around. The bird was bright red with a frill on its head; it's called a cardinal. It twittered at me, cocking its head back and forth, and then it flew away, albeit awkwardly.

It was great to see the life cycles within the aquaponics green-house. Understanding how each plant or animal served a purpose was mind-blowing. I can see that God designed it all, that He created the beautiful world where my own parents once lived, even though I have never seen the spectacular and wild plants and animals of Earth.

I know some people don't recognize Creation as the work of God because they believe that evolution has the power to create without His direction. The Evolts, who will be arriving in a few days, have that view.

My dad has explained the central ideas of evolution to me, pointing out the gaps and weaknesses in a theory that suggests that the diversity of life on Earth is essentially a big, incredible accident with no input from our Creator. But it is easy for me to look at all the life around me and appreciate its diversity and design. I know that we have been designed intelligently and with a clear purpose. A purpose I learn about a little more each day out here in the dark depths of the galaxy.

IIIIIIIIIIFAITH AT THE EDGE: CREATION

The first chapter of Genesis is a fantastic description of God at work, creating everything from the land to the skies. The sun, the moon, the stars. All the plants and animals. And then humans.

And what an amazingly designed system! Every creature He designed and every flower He painted serves a purpose. For example, did you know that ladybugs eat aphids, preventing the little bugs from eating too many leaves on plants? And have you heard about the kapok tree? This gargantuan tree grows deep in Earth's rain forest, providing a home for hundreds of animals and insects.

Even more amazing is that God wants people to partner with Him, to maintain what He started. God invited Adam to use his own creativity to name the animals. In the same way, God invites you to use your creativity in this world to be stewards of His Creation, whether that's at school, in your work, anywhere! What an honor it is to partner with God, the Creator of the universe.

EXPLORATION ----------------------

1. Take some time to read Genesis 1:1–2:3. Then, the next time you are outside, write about the beauty you see in the world God created. Reflect on some ideas about how you can continue to care and steward His creation, using the creativity God gave you.

2. Recognize the beauty and diversity of God's design by creating a list of the things you observe as you go on a walk, take a hike, or sit by the window. What can you learn about God from His Creation?

"**D**ad, CB-21 is off course by one hundred meters," I reported. Even though I was talking to my dad, we were in the Titan Operations Command Module conducting an official maneuver between one of the settlement's constructo-bots and the orbital station, which meant following every protocol, including verbal ones.

"Switch to manual override," my dad said.

"Roger," I said. I swiped my finger across the words "auto docking engaged." The text switched momentarily to "manual docking engaged," but then it suddenly changed back. I tried swiping again, and then a third and fourth time. The display kept showing that CB-21 was set to auto dock.

"Gavin, status?" my dad asked me.

"Auto to manual switch not remaining in effect," I said.

My dad was over my shoulder a second later. He tried the process with the same results.

"Aurora, can you confirm CB-21's current proximity to *Provider*?" Dad asked.

"Confirmed, one hundred meters off course, with a meter-per-minute drift," my sister reported.

"All right, time for action. Gavin, come with me to Airlock C," he said.

As we approached the airlock, my knees wobbled, my breathing sped up, and my forehead perspired. I reached out to balance myself against the wall of the swirling corridor.

"Dad," I said.

He turned, then jogged back to me. "Gavin, are you okay?"

I shook my head. "I feel dizzy. Woozy. Is the ship twisting?"

"No." Dad raised his mTalk, "Nebula and Comet, can you come to Airlock C's corridor?"

Dad helped me sit. "Put your head between your legs." He put his arm around me and rubbed my back in slow, methodical circles. "It's all right, Gavin. Breathe deep."

I closed my eyes and breathed.

"What happened?" Dad asked.

I shook my head. "I don't know."

"I think I might," my dad said. "Your last experience outside *Provider* was pretty traumatic. It was scary for me to just hear it over the comms, so I am sure it was terrifying for you."

I nodded.

"And so, if you aren't ready to go out there yet, I'll understand," he said. "But if you do go, you'll be overcoming your fear."

I pictured that moment a few days ago when my walker-suit

was punctured. I again felt the anxiety of not having enough time to make it back to the airlock before running out of oxygen. Once again, I heard KEWD's robotic warnings in my mind. But then I recalled my mom's calming voice, the way she encouraged me to trust God and remember my training. Not only had I prepared for situations like the one I experienced, but I had a greater power watching over me, protecting me. I imagined several angels floating nearby me outside the station.

Was that really what it was like?

"Dad, have you ever experienced something like what I did?"

My dad nodded. "I was on Mars Orbital Station 2—the one that orbited the planet as a supply depot for ships headed back to Earth or Luna. I conducted extensive spacewalks on the orbital platform to maintain the solar panels and the many airlocks used for loading and offloading cargo and supplies."

Dad looked away as he recalled the memory. "One day, the AI that was docking the shuttle from Mars to the station suddenly went offline, and the shuttle rammed into one of the airlocks. I was called out to help rescue the pilot and passengers. While we were conducting the rescue, a jagged part of the ship caught on my ExoSuit, snagging a hole in the outer layer. I got a series of alerts in rapid succession. The airlock that we were closest to was still unusable due to the incident. So, like you, I was required to use an emergency patch. I then had to enter the shuttle through its airlock and wait for the rescue mission to finish, becoming one of the stranded crew on the shuttle myself."

My dad took a deep breath. "I'll never forget that moment, but I did learn two things. One was the value of the training that we do. Second, I learned that my father had prayed for me every day of my life. I had a message from him that I received when I got back to our cabin after the ordeal. It said, 'Son, I felt an urgent need to pray for you again today. I hope you are doing well. Know that I love you and pray for your safety each and every day.'"

"Wow," I said. "Really?"

"Yes, Gavin. God is always with us. What's more, His Holy Spirit often prompts us when we need to pray," my dad said. "That's what your grandfather did: he was prompted, and so right then and there, he prayed. Some may call this foolishness, but I have felt and seen prayer's efficacy firsthand, both in my life and in the lives of you kids. Your mom and I also pray for you each and every day."

I had heard several stories about my dad's tours on the Mars orbital station, and I knew my grandfather was a man of prayer, but I'd never heard that connection before.

My mom and Comet both arrived at that moment.

"What is it, Dad?" Comet asked.

Dad looked at me; I nodded. "Nothing. Gavin's all right now." Dad offered me his hand. "Help us with our suits."

My mom looked knowingly at me, but she smiled with confidence.

A few minutes later, the airlock opened, and the dark empty space was before me. After a long breath, I stepped out from the airlock. Then with a tap on my controls, the thrusters on my J-Pak fired, and I cruised out toward the broken constructo-bot. I was okay.

I can do this. God is with me.

‖‖‖FAITH AT THE EDGE: OVERCOMING FEAR

The idea of going out to face the dangers of open space again nearly crippled Gavin with fear. He couldn't move. He couldn't breathe. And he felt like he was all by himself in this fear. Feeling alone often makes it easy for fear to seem overwhelming.

Gavin's fear was triggered by his memories of the last time he was on a spacewalk, the time he'd accidentally torn a hole in his walker-suit. The fear of a repeat incident—of losing oxygen and facing the possibility of death—overwhelmed him. Gavin had forgotten one very important detail though. He wasn't really alone. His dad *was* with him.

And you are never alone either. When Moses was old and knew he could not lead Israel anymore, he encouraged Joshua to "be strong and courageous" as he was taking over the job. Moses told Joshua that God would always be with him: "It is the LORD who goes before you. He will be with you; he will not leave you or forsake you. Do not fear or be dismayed" (Deuteronomy 31:7-8).

It can be so easy to forget that God is with you when you're about to face a frightening situation. When those challenges come up, remind yourself that God cares about you, He loves you, and He is with you.

Be strong and courageous. It is the Lord who goes before you.

EXPLORATION -

1. God doesn't want us to constantly live in fear. The Bible frequently tells us, "Do not be afraid," yet fear is a real emotion that God gave us so that we don't rush into potentially dangerous situations. What are you afraid of? Why do you think you have this kind of fear?

2. Have you ever had to overcome a fear in order to accomplish something? What did you do to overcome that fear?

3. Have you ever received help just when you needed it—and then you later discovered that someone had been praying for you?

"Inspire operational systems check in progress," Aurora said.

"Good," my dad said. "Gavin, what is the status of the solar field?"

"Solar field operational, functioning at 98 percent capacity."

"Excellent. Comet, what's the status on the constructo-bot fleet?"

"All c-bots operational," Comet replied.

"Dad," Aurora interrupted. "Receiving a failure notification for airlock five. But no indication of depressurization or atmospheric leak."

My dad's eyebrows furrowed, his lips a thin tight line. He tapped the screen before him, likely reading the status report Aurora had received from KEWD.

He tapped some more, then called my mom over. She looked over the screen and frowned. Then she nodded. The silent exchange was digging at me. Whatever was happening certainly didn't seem good. And that was bad because tomorrow we were supposed to take the lander *Hopper* down to the surface of Titan and spend our first night in the settlement's hab-dome.

We ran the operational systems check two more times, each with the same result.

"Comet, scrub the Titan landing mission from tomorrow's schedule," my dad ordered.

"What! Why?" I asked.

"Gavin, we are on a mission," my dad said. This meant we are to use proper procedural language.

"Um . . . why are we scrubbing the lander mission?" I asked, even though I already knew the reason.

"We cannot risk the entire crew to a failed airlock," my dad said.

I didn't respond again. I'd been looking forward to this day, the day we as a family would begin our life on Titan permanently. We'd spent years preparing. Up until now, only my dad, mom, and Comet had been down to Titan.

"Okay, mission scrubbed," Comet said.

"Confirmed, mission cancelled," my dad said.

The disappointment hit me like the g-force from a Martian takeoff. "Dad, may I be dismissed?"

Everyone looked at me. But I knew that with tomorrow's mission off, there wasn't anything more for me to do right now. There would be more systems checks and problem-solving regarding Inspire, but none of it had to do with my area of specialization.

"Yes, dismissed," my dad said. I marched from the Titan Operations Command Module without another word.

I intended to head to our cabin, but I ended up at the observatory module, which is called the Titan Observation Port. This module has a row of windows with a perfect view of Titan. From here, I could see Inspire—well, at least I could with the help of a digital overlay that used various data streams to create a live video image of the new settlement. In an emergency, the crew of *Provider* could watch from here for electromagnetic signals, which serve as a form of emergency communication. Redundancy is the name of the game in space life. For every task, we have a backup plan in case something goes wrong with a primary system.

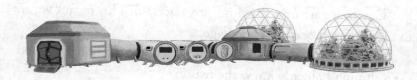

I imagined again the moment of stepping from *Hopper* onto the surface of Titan. Neither Aurora nor I had been there yet— only my dad, mom, and Comet had made the trip down. Looking out at Titan, the moon felt so close, yet it was totally out of my grasp. And while I understood that my dad was only trying to keep us safe, it was still hard to accept the postponement of the landing. I'd been looking forward to this day since we first left Mars—before we even arrived on *Provider*. I could imagine what Aurora would say: "What's a few more days added on to six years?"

My answer to that? "I know I'm learning patience, sure, but what about *disappointment*? That's real too."

"Hello, Gavin." It was Ms. Carver, *Provider*'s Chief Engineer. I hadn't seen her over at the side of the observation module. "I'm sorry to hear about your mission."

The crew already knows? I wondered. Well, maybe not the whole crew. My dad had probably told Ms. Carver about the mission cancellation so they could discuss a course of action.

I shrugged. "Yes, ma'am, it is unfortunate."

She laughed kindly. "Gavin, it's fine—you can be at ease."

I sighed. "Okay."

"You know, I've been working in space for more than thirty years," Ms. Carver said. "I've had my share of setbacks—and I recognize disappointment all too well." Her smile was one of understanding. "And it is okay to be disappointed, Gavin. Your feelings are natural, so don't let anyone try to tell you otherwise."

I sighed again and nodded. "Yes, I know."

She turned toward the door. I expected she was going to the Titan Operations Command Module to meet with Dad about the airlock problem. But she stopped first and looked back at me. "But what matters, Gavin, is what you do next—how you move past those feelings. You've always been upbeat. Find your way back soon. You don't want the cloud of disappointment to steal your joy for too long."

As she left, she began to whistle her favorite tune. It was a very old song, one my mom had sung to me when I was younger: *Apple Red Happiness.* I recalled some of the lyrics:

> Throw away your sin, let God's love shine in.
> Try it and you'll see how you get
> Apple red happiness.

I looked out the windows again. Titan, the great yellowish orb, stood before me in all its glory. *Well, I'll be there soon,* I thought.

Maybe I could take Ms. Carver's advice and spread cheer and joy instead of melancholy. My family might appreciate that. They were probably disappointed too.

IIIIIIIIII FaITH aT THE EDGE: DEaLING WITH DISaPPOINTMENT

Ms. Carver has seen a lot during her years in space, and she has learned something Gavin is just starting to realize: Disappointment comes to every person at some point. Life is complicated, with a multitude of variables impossible for any human—or AI, for that matter—to predict or control. Disappointment often sets in when a desired or expected outcome fails to happen. Sometimes the feelings of disappointment can be so strong that it seems as if nothing good will ever happen again.

Hiding or ignoring disappointment will not help us deal with it. As Ms. Carver said, disappointment is a natural feeling, just as many other emotions are. But at the same time, disappointment should not permanently control all of our thoughts and actions. There are ways to work through disappointment and have joy again.

In Psalm 42, the disappointed and distressed author reminds himself to place his hope in God, who is his salvation. Indeed, God is the one constant among the ever-changing variables of life, and He will never fail to keep His promises. God's promise in Romans 8:28 is particularly comforting when life brings disappointments: God is in control and can bring good things out of the most disappointing events! Now that is a reason to have joy.

And we know that for those who love God all things work together for good, for those who are called according to his purpose.

—ROMANS 8:28

EXPLORATION -

1. Can you recall a time when you've been very disappointed because something didn't turn out like you'd expected? If so, how did you handle it?

2. Have you ever been disappointed by something but then it ended up working out better than you had expected?

3. Read Psalm 42. What could you do to remind yourself of God and His promises when you're disappointed?

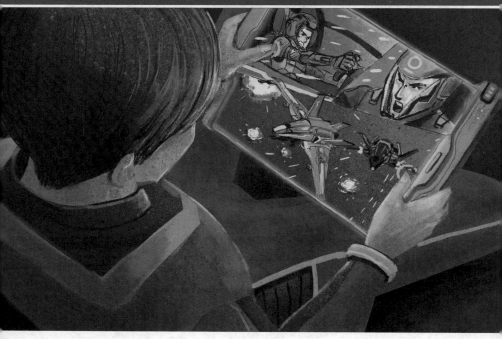

"It's going to be a few days at least," my dad said over the comms. First thing this morning, Dad took *Hopper* to Titan's surface. It was a flawless entry and landing. Visual inspection of Inspire was good, but when my dad attempted to use Airlock 5 (the one reporting an issue) to gain access to the hab-dome, it would not open or even respond. He had to access Inspire from Airlock 3 on the eastern side of the settlement. But when he did this, he got an alert reporting that Airlock 2 had also opened simultaneously! Something was seriously amiss.

The airlocks keep the breathable air inside the settlement so that it won't escape into Titan's atmosphere. They also stop poisonous gases from entering the settlement. So if someone had been in Airlock 2 removing their TerraSuit (the suits we'll use during terrestrial movement on Titan) when this malfunction occurred, they could have died when all the breathable air escaped outside.

Hopper

"Phoenix, what's causing the issue?" Mom asked.

"Looks like the central control node was wired incorrectly," my dad explained. "A quantex-node module is routing several ion connections. I'll have to disconnect them all and reconnect, but I'll have to do a bypass first. I may need you or Comet to help me."

"Right," my mom said.

I looked over at Comet. He had a big grin on his face. He would likely get to go down to Titan. That didn't seem fair. But I quickly shoved the thought aside. This wasn't about fairness—this was about Comet's specialization. He was trained to handle this job.

"Okay, well, I believe it would make sense to send Comet so I can remain behind with Aurora and Gavin," Mom said.

There was a moment's pause.

"Comet, have you completed your quantex-node certification?" my dad asked.

Comet's smile disappeared. "No, sir," he said.

I admit my mouth twitched into a slight smile at that.

"Then I guess, Nebula, it will need to be you," my dad said jovially. "It'll be like a little vacation, the kind we took before the kids arrived."

My mom laughed. "Roger that. When will you return on *Hopper*?"

"I'll prep the lander now. No point in wasting time; there isn't much for me to do unless I have assistance," my dad explained. "KEWD says my ETA is three hours."

"I'll be ready. Command out," my mom said, then turned to us. "*Beyond* will be here in only a few days, so I want you to help the crew finish preparing for the arrival of the Evolt and Waves families. I'll let Commander Pujols know." She lifted her mTalk. "And I want your absolute best behaviors."

"Mom, perhaps we should *all* go to Inspire. I mean, we were going to go yesterday, and nearly half our team will be there," I said. "The crew doesn't really need us to finish getting ready or help show the new families around. KEWD could even take them on a guided tour with their mTalks."

Mom put her hands on my shoulders and looked into my eyes. "Gavin, we must follow safety procedures, and with any sort of system failure our policy is to minimize the risk exposure to the team. The three of you are not necessary to this mission, and therefore your presence is an unnecessary risk to your lives."

"But we could . . ."

"Listen, we will get this solved quickly, and your dad and I will be taking extra precautions while we are there to ensure we are safe," my mom said. Then she pulled my head down and kissed my forehead. "You'll be fine here."

She released me, "Now I need to go find Commander Pujols. I'll meet you all back in our cabin."

The second Mom was gone, Comet laughed. "Scared to have Mom and Dad on another planet, Gavin?" he jeered. "Poor baby."

"It's a moon, Comet," Aurora shot back. She was looking down at a screen, reading something.

Unfazed, I approached my brother. I was taller than him, after all. "I'm not scared of Mom and Dad being away," I told him.

Comet snickered, but he turned from me and faced his console again. "Then what are you scared of?"

"Nothing," I said, walking out toward our cabin. I grabbed my mTab and dropped into one of the air loungers to read my favorite comic series, *Cosmic Corsairs*. KEWD had notified me that the latest issue had finally arrived. The story was set far off on Alpha Centauri. Humans haven't reached that star system in real life yet, but these comics are pretty exciting—sort of like the old stories from Earth about the American Wild West or the Caribbean Sea filled with pirates. (I only know about those stories from my history courses.)

About a half-hour later, the hatch to our cabin opened and Mom walked in.

"Hey, Gavin, is everything alright?" she asked.

I shrugged.

"Your dad and I won't be gone that long, and we'll be safe. I prom—"

"It's not that, Mom," I said.

"Oh, then what?"

"Well . . ." I was actually too embarrassed to say what I was thinking about. And I doubt she expected it.

"Gavin, no secrets. You can tell me anything," she said.

"It's *Beyond*. It's arriving soon, and I was . . . well, I was hoping we'd already be on Titan when it did," I explained. "I'm not sure about these people—I mean meeting these people."

"We've been on several vid-chats with them, and they are all quite friendly," my mom said.

"I know, and they've been selected based on personality and skillset matches so that the three families will function cohesively within the settlement," I rattled off. "But what if . . . ?" I paused and stared ferociously at my hands. "What if they don't like me? What if they don't like any of us?"

My mom came to my side and pulled my chin up, so I was looking up at her now.

"Gavin, you are a brilliant, kind, courteous, and witty young man," my mom said. "If you be you, *you* can't lose."

"Well, you're my mom," I said. "You have to say that."

"Yes, it's my greatest privilege—being your mom. I see you at your best and in your struggles. I know you. I know what's in there," she said, pointing at my chest. "You have a heart of gold and a wit that can make anyone smile."

I felt myself blush at her words.

"Thanks, Mom," I said. She pulled me up from my chair and gave me a hug.

"You're an ambassador here. The two families coming have never been this far from Earth, and they've never lived on a station for more than a few days. They've always lived terrestrially on either Earth or Mars. It'll be good to have someone courageous, optimistic, and experienced like you to greet them and help them get their space legs."

"Alright, Mom, I'll do it. I'll be the best ambassador I can be." Then I smirked. "Yeah, I guess I would be better at this than KEWD . . . it would be pretty hard for an AI stuck in a computer to demonstrate what it means to have space legs."

Mom winked at me. "You got that right. Now, help me pack up some of my gear," she said.

IIIIIFaiTH aT THe eDGe: seCuRiTY

Many people feel nervous when facing new people and new situations. Why is that?

In this case, Gavin was nervous because he was insecure about his own identity and self-worth. He wasn't confident in his value as a person, and that caused him to fear that the newcomers wouldn't like or accept him. His mom helped him overcome those feelings by reassuring him of his true worth and value.

Emotions like anxiety and fear can have a way of clouding the truth about a situation, so sometimes it takes a person with an unclouded view of the situation to guide you away from anxiety and help you see what's really true. But choose your guide wisely! Don't believe everything other people tell you about yourself. Some people are deceived themselves, and they may steer you in the wrong direction or tell you lies about who you are. Gavin chose wisely when he listened to his mom, because she knows and loves him.

Of course, the One with the most accurate view of who you are is always God. He created you, and He is pleased with you. You are His precious child, and no one knows you better than He does. How precious are you? God says that the death of Jesus on the cross was a price worth paying to redeem you from sin. He loves and values you that much! Recognizing who you are in God's eyes—and choosing to believe in His love for you—will give you more confidence and security than anyone or anything else.

> For while we were still weak, at the right time Christ died for the ungodly. For one will scarcely die for a righteous person—though perhaps for a good person one would dare even to die—but God shows his love for us in that while we were still sinners, Christ died for us.
>
> —ROMANS 5:6-8

EXPLORATION ----------------------

1. Have you ever been nervous about meeting new people or facing a new situation? Why do you think the situation caused you to be anxious?

2. Has someone ever reassured you like Gavin's mom reassured him? How do the words of a trusted guide help us to face life's challenges?

3. Read 1 Peter 2:9 and Jeremiah 1:5. How does God's love and acceptance and knowledge of you make you feel? How might this affect the choices you make in daily life?

"No, there, Aurora," Comet ordered. "The nano-fuse has to be inverted."

Aurora glared at Comet. Then she twisted her Magnilox to release the nano-fuse and reinsert it the other way. "It looks the same on both sides."

"It's not," Comet said sternly. "It needs to be inserted correctly. And you're taking too long."

KEWD piped up from mTalk on Aurora's wrist, "She has been working on this particular fuse for 1.45 minutes."

"See? Don't rush me," Aurora said.

"Well, do it right the first time," Comet responded.

"Comet, don't be so bossy," I said.

"I'm mission lead."

"Doesn't mean you have to be rude," I retorted.

"Gavin, just zip it," Comet said. "That's an order."

I raised my mTalk. "KEWD, end simulation." The Titan surface dissolved around us.

"What was that?" Comet said. "We aren't finished."

"I am done until you stop being so controlling," I said.

Aurora sighed and shook her head. "Gavin's right."

"Mom told us to do this training," Comet said.

"But she didn't say for you to be so bossy," Aurora argued.

"So, it's two against one," Comet said.

"Looks that way," I said.

"Fine," Comet said. He stormed out of the virtual reality pod.

"He's going to call Mom," I said.

"No, he won't," Aurora said. "His pride won't let him admit failure. He won't want them to know he wasn't able to lead us or handle the situation."

"True," I said. I glanced at the clock on my mTalk. "What about lunch? I'm starving."

"Me too. What's that, like, the fifth simulation we've run today?" Aurora asked.

"Yeah, at least."

We left the simulation pod and headed for the galley. "I wonder what Chef Raytza created today."

"I hope it's not something too inventive," I said. "I know she's a space chef, but she sure takes out-of-this-world recipes to a new level. And not always in a good way."

"It's not her fault," Aurora said. "Well, not all the time. I mean, the produce from the aquaponics greenhouse doesn't always develop as expected. And we've been waiting a long time for the new supply shipment."

"You can't blame all the flavors on supply chain issues," I said. "I mean, the guava and goat cheese empanadas were spectacular, but the bean sprout and banana casserole totally missed the mark."

As we approached the galley, we detected a rather . . . well, *unique* smell. And when we got to the counter, the look was also unique.

"Hola, Greystones," Raytza said. "Fish and garbanzo bean pie, with sweet chili sauce."

I forced a smile. "Great," I said.

"Gavin, it may be an odd combination, but we're out of many of my regular ingredients," Raytza said with a smile. "And Dr. Sprucevine hasn't been able to get all the herbs I need to grow in the aquaponics greenhouse."

Aurora smiled. "Not all plants take to space very well."

Raytza nodded. "We all just have to have a bit of patience while waiting for the arrival of our supplies as well as the growth of the right plants."

"And with getting to the surface," I said.

"I heard about the delay in going to Inspire," Raytza said. "I'm sure you are all disappointed. It's hard to find ways to remain patient and occupy our minds with something else. Our minds get stuck on the problem. I imagine that's making life pretty stressful."

Instantly, I thought of my brother, Comet.

"You said that right," I said. I took my tray of food to a nearby table and sat down with Aurora. I had an unpleasant feeling in my stomach, and it wasn't hunger.

I tapped my mTalk. "Hey, Comet, will you join us for lunch?" Aurora gave me a questioning look.

A second passed, and then there was a hesitant response. "Sure," Comet said.

A few minutes later, Comet arrived. I'd already gotten him a tray of food, so he sat down.

"Comet, I'm sorry," I said. "I know you're just trying to lead us in training, and I also know you're as disappointed as I am that we didn't get to go to Titan."

Comet nodded. "I'm sorry too. I know I was a bit over the top earlier. You are right—I am disappointed, but disappointment doesn't excuse my attitude. I'm supposed to be a leader, and a good leader needs to have patience and find ways to be encouraging. We were just training. I didn't need to be rude. Forgive me?"

"Of course," I said.

Aurora looked up. "Comet, of course I do. But that nano-fuse really does work either way."

The three of us laughed.

"And now, let's make the best of *this*—whatever it is," I said, turning toward my lunch. I waited for a second longer than my siblings, and their reactions told me that, even with the odd combination of ingredients, Raytza had crafted a winning recipe.

IIIIIIIIFAITH AT THE EDGE: PATIENCE

Waiting for something can be difficult, especially when emotions are already taut from stress or disappointment. Then it becomes that much easier for our self-control to break down. We may snap at each other like the Greystone siblings did today.

As Paul notes in Ephesians, we are to bear with one another in love with patience and gentleness if we are to maintain peace and unity. When Comet treated his siblings rudely instead of with gentleness and patience, it created a division between them. It kept them from working well as a team to complete their training.

> I therefore, a prisoner for the Lord, urge you to walk in a manner worthy of the calling to which you have been called, with all humility and gentleness, with patience, bearing with one another in love, eager to maintain the unity of the Spirit in the bond of peace.
>
> —EPHESIANS 4:1-3

Impatience tends to focus the mind on whatever is going wrong, blocking out other considerations. Maybe that's why Chef Raytza explained that being patient often involves finding different ways to occupy the mind. If something fails to work out, we find something else to focus on instead of remaining frustrated about the failure. That something else may be pretty simple—like Chef Raytza's fish with garbanzo bean pie, a pleasant surprise for the Greystone siblings.

Other times, stepping away from the stressful challenge for a time can help bring a new understanding to the situation. As he talked with Chef Raytza, Gavin was able to see past Comet's pride and rudeness because he recognized that his brother was struggling with the same disappointment he was.

EXPLORATION -

1. When is it most difficult for you to be patient? What could you do to develop more patience in that situation?

2. Read James 1:2-4. Though it sometimes seems as though a challenge is unendurable and will never end, God can use it to build patience, to perfect your character. What may help you take your mind off your problem and instead rejoice in what He is doing?

"If we can find a way to more rapidly drill through Titan's rock-ice surface to reach the subsurface ocean, we can provide increased liquid H20 for the settlement," Dr. Helios explained at his million-miles-a-minute, highly caffeinated pace. "I believe the following combination will allow us to quickly dissolve the surface ice, speeding up our access to the subsurface ocean. We can then utilize our advanced desalination process to create clean water for drinking and for growing plants."

Dr. Helios tapped his screen, and an outline appeared on my mTab. "You'll note I am utilizing organic substrates and liquids readily available on the surface of Titan," he continued. "The secret sauce, as I like to call it, is this Nano-bionetics injector that will guide the drill head through the surface while providing a steady flow of the organic solution."

As usual, keeping up with the larger-than-life (and perhaps not even real) words of Dr. Helios was a challenge, but at least I had instructions on my mTab as well as KEWD, who was adept at translating Dr. Helios into normal-human language.

Dr. Helios pointed to a storage locker. "Gavin, I have tested this solution on a very small scale, but we are about to test it on a much grander scale. It's time to get into our Bliz-Zero Gear and begin. The temperature inside the cryo-storage is set to -290°F, the temperature of the surface of Titan."

We suited up, and Dr. Helios led me to a large cryo-storage unit at the back of the laboratory. He punched in the code, and the hatch slid open as a burst of whitish gas flowed outward like a storm cloud. Inside was a gargantuan piece of rock-ice.

"How'd you get that?" I asked.

"I crafted it," Dr. Helios said. "This is two thousand gallons of water frozen to perfect, rock-solid ice, an exact match to the ice you'll experience on the surface of Titan," he said.

Two thousand gallons of water in space is a whole lot of water. I was staring at the reason for our recently mandated water and energy conservation rules.

"Now, I have already placed the ionic drill above the ice," Dr. Helios continued. "But we need to deliver the organic solution through the Nano-bionetics injector. I will be here at the controls while you monitor the solution delivery and the progress of the drill down through the ice surface. You'll be up there." He pointed to a large metal walkway suspended above the ice block. "We will also use a suction system to extract the liquid water. And I must note, it is very, very important that the extracted liquid be contained, or it could increase the melt rate of the rock-ice." Dr. Helios smiled at me through his helmet visor. "Are you ready?"

I nodded. "Yes, sir."

"Then take your position on the walkway," he said. I climbed up and positioned myself near the drill's targeted entry point.

"Lowering drill," he added.

A purple light on the drill pulsed as it spun and lowered toward the massive block of ice. I realized then that this block of ice took up nearly three-quarters of the room, and it was much taller than it was wide.

"Activate the Nano-bionetics injector."

The good doctor had not actually explained how to do that yet, but I saw a trigger on a control stick and pulled it. A light blinked, and a hose wiggled a bit as solution began to flow through it and down to the drill.

A dozen minutes passed. I observed the drill very slowly creeping down through the block of ice.

"Excellent, it's working," Dr. Helios said. "We've only just begun, and we're at a 15 percent increase in drill speed rate."

BEEP BEEP

Dr. Helios looked down at his mTalk. "Oh, well, that can't . . . hmm. Gavin, I am needed in the Command Module. Can you monitor the progress?" Dr. Helios asked, already exiting the cryo-storage. He stopped and then turned. "Just . . . watch the saturation levels. Make sure the rock-ice isn't melting at an unsustainable rate. Maintain the current speed."

"But . . ." And then he was gone. I climbed down from the walkway to check the monitoring station. All the bars and graphs were green. *That's good, right?*

"KEWD," I said into my mTalk. "You know anything about this experiment?"

"Yes, I helped develop the procedure and the monitoring application," the AI said.

"Great, let me know if any of these numbers get out of the safe range. I'll keep watching from the walkway," I said.

The drill was humming along, and the depth seemed to be increasing, but it was painstakingly slow, and my Bliz-Zero parka was itchy. Maybe I could speed this up a bit—just a *tiny* bit. It shouldn't hurt anything. The experiment appeared highly stable.

I pulled the trigger on the controls to increase the solution delivery. The hose shook a little as the rate of flow increased. I looked down the hole; everything seemed good.

"KEWD, any change in drill speed rate?"

"Ten percent increase," KEWD said. That was good. More solution meant quicker drilling. My parka was really bugging me—I was beginning to feel warm. *How much longer would this take?*

I pulled the trigger again, and the hose writhed a bit. It alarmed me for a moment, but then it seemed to settle into a rhythm.

"KEWD, any change in drill speed rate?"

"Ten percent increase," KEWD explained.

So, with each pull of the trigger, we gained a 10 percent speed increase.

I stepped down from the walkway to look at the block of ice. I couldn't quite make out the position of the drill because the ice wasn't transparent enough, but I estimated it was about halfway through the block of ice. I glanced at my mTalk. I'd been at this for more than half an hour. I climbed back up on the walkway and peered into the hole. There was liquid in the hole surrounding the drill.

Where was that liquid coming from? It took a moment for me to realize that I hadn't increased the suction to remove the additional liquid.

"KEWD, increase suction by 20 percent," I said.

"Suction increased."

The other hose, which I assumed was the one removing the liquid, rattled and quivered. I climbed down to look at the ice block again. This time, I could see a dark shape within the ice. It wasn't there before, and the outline of the dark shape seemed to be growing.

"KEWD, pause drill," I said, and the drill stopped spinning. I went back to the walkway and looked down the hole. The liquid was rising up the hole slowly.

"KEWD, deactivate the Nano-bionetics injector. Increase suction."

"Deactivation not successful," KEWD relayed. "Suction increased."

The solution delivery hose continued to vibrate, liquid clearly flowing down into the drill hole. The suction line began to shake, and not just a little, but a lot.

POW! Woosh!

A spray of liquid solution shot from a crack halfway up the pipe. The liquid rained down across the surface of the rock-ice block. The result was instant; pockmarks formed on the surface of the ice as the water melted and pooled. The solution delivery and suction both continued.

"KEWD, activate emergency shutdown!" I shouted.

"The protocols for emergency shutdown include completely shutting down power to the chamber and to the equipment," KEWD said.

"Do it! Emergency shutdown now," I said.

The emergency red lights flickered on, the drill stopped, the suction stopped.

I walked around the block of ice. The black blob within was still growing, and now there was water slowly trickling down the side of the block of ice.

"Chamber temperature increasing," KEWD warned.

"What, why?"

"Emergency shutoff deactivated chamber cooling system and activated safety venting," KEWD said.

The cryo-refrigeration had ceased. So not only was the chamber not being cooled, but all the cold air was being evacuated from the chamber. Worse, the solution Dr. Helios had concocted was still doing its work, accelerating the melting of the ice block at the surface and within.

The blob within the block broke free, and liquid gushed out into the chamber. Too much of the solution had been released and too much had remained in the chamber. The block appeared to sink into the floor, and the water level in the chamber began to rise. I trudged through the water and slush and climbed up onto the metal walkway as the room began to fill around me.

I knew the room was larger than the amount of water, so the chamber would not fill all the way, but it was still a terrifying reality as the water rose around me.

Then, suddenly, the hatch to the chamber opened, and water gushed out the entrance. I heard the shout of Dr. Helios before seeing him swept away from the opening.

Within a moment, only an inch or so of liquid remained across the chamber floor. I stepped through the water and went out to find Dr. Helios. He was sopping wet and piping mad.

"What on Titan have you done, Greystone?"

"Well . . ." I took a deep breath. "I'm sorry." I pulled Dr. Helios to his feet. "The solution worked."

"I see that," his tone changed. "But my calculations were quite specific to ensure a correlation between solution delivery and extraction."

"Sir, I might have slightly increased the delivery speed," I explained. "But I also increased suction."

Dr. Helios slipped his mTab out of the satchel he had over his shoulder. Liquid dripped from the device, but its screen still glowed. "Ah, but your percentages were wrong. Ten percent on top of 10 percent is not the same as 20 percent."

"Also, the extraction line sprung a leak," KEWD added.

Dr. Helios shook his head. "Well, I'm not happy with your lack of following instructions, but you can't take all the blame. I did leave without providing specific instruction." He trudged through the liquid slush and to the wall, where he removed a vacuum-like device. "Let's get this cleaned up together."

"Yes, sir," I said.

"Gavin, I'm glad you're curious, but in the future, direct your curiosity through me first," he said.

"Yes, sir."

IIIIIFAITH AT THE EDGE: FOLLOWING INSTRUCTIONS

Left to monitor the drilling by himself, Gavin Greystone learned a valuable lesson about following the instructions given by a leader. Gavin's experience is similar to the account of King Saul in the Old Testament. In 1 Samuel 15, God gave Saul specific instructions for how to handle war with the

Amalekites. Saul followed part but not all of God's instructions. So God told the prophet Samuel: "I regret that I have made Saul king, for he has turned back from following me and has not performed my commandments" (1 Samuel 15:11).

Saul lost his kingdom, but the consequences of his disobedience reached far beyond himself. Indeed, Saul's disobedience likely contributed to the attempted murder of God's people, the Jews. Haman, the man who tried to kill all of the Jews in Persia during Queen Esther's rule, was a descendent of Agag, the king of the Amalekites in Saul's day (Esther 3:1).

God does not give instructions without a good reason. The same is true of wise people in authority. At times, that reason may not be apparent, but it still exists. Not knowing the bigger picture as God did, Saul relied on his own limited knowledge and acted disobediently with nearly fatal consequences.

By disregarding the instructions of Dr. Helios—who had many years of scientific training and was in charge of the drilling test—Gavin created a large mess. Yes, he would have had to endure the drill test (not to mention his itchy parka) a little longer, but things would have gone far better for Gavin if he'd recognized the importance of following wise instructions.

Whoever scorns instruction will pay for it, but whoever respects a command is rewarded.
—PROVERBS 13:13, NIV

> Whoever gives heed to instruction prospers, and blessed is the one who trusts in the LORD.
>
> **—PROVERBS 16:20, NIV**

EXPLORATION ----------------------

1. Was there ever a time when you didn't follow instructions? What happened as a result?

2. Read 2 Timothy 3:16. When Christians are unsure of what to do, where do they find their instructions? Why is it important to follow these instructions?

"**D**ocking in three, two, one," KEWD said. There was a slight *clank*, and then: "*Beyond* docking successful. Airlock secure in thirty seconds."

I looked at Comet. We were both fully uniformed in our hab-suits and ready to welcome our guests: two new families who would later join us on Titan as the beginning of a new settlement. This was the first step in the team coming together.

"Gavin, prepare to release the hatch lock on my count. Three, two, one, *release*," Comet said. We both pulled the release lever, and the hatch door shifted inward.

Comet then pulled on the handle, and the door swung open. At first, there was no one there. Then two helmeted heads popped into view. I recognized the two faces from the vid-chats—Orbitus and Solar, the two Waves teens.

"Well, here we are," Orbitus said. He gave each of us a smile.

"Indeed, we are here," added Solar with a laugh.

"I'm Comet," my brother said, extending a gloved hand. But Orbitus didn't take it. Instead, he pulled himself through the hatch.

Solar did take my brother's hand as she climbed through the hatch. "Wow, it's smaller than I imagined."

My brother shot me a glance.

"I'm kidding," Solar said. "I know this is just the airlock."

Two more figures stepped into view. "Orbitus, retrieve your luggage and Solar's, too."

I nodded. "Nice to meet you in person finally. I am Gavin Greystone."

"And I am Comet Greystone, senior member of the Greystones on *Provider* while our parents are on Inspire."

I nearly choked. Comet was certainly ensuring that I knew the chain of command.

"Pleasure to finally meet you both," Mrs. Waves said with a kind smile. "I am grateful you were able to remain on the platform during our arrival."

Comet nodded. Neither he nor I really wanted to still be here. We should have already been on Titan. But I knew that Mrs. Waves meant well.

"Yes, unfortunate about the malfunction," Mr. Waves said. "I do hope it does not delay our arrival to Titan. We've already spent far too much time in space."

The Waveses were scientists from Mars who had spent all their time in Falcon Settlement. The trip from Mars to Titan was their first spacefaring mission in seven years.

"Welcome aboard!" Comet said. "Now, if you could step toward the back of the airlock while we greet the Evolts, it would be much appreciated."

Solar Waves and her parents moved toward the back. I could hear them chatting.

Next, a visor filled with fiery red hair came into view: Lilly Evolt. Based on our vid-chats, I suspected Lilly Evolt was easily the most energetic person I had ever met. Her smile was bright, and she had bright green eyes that contrasted with her flaming red hair.

"Gavin," she squealed as she climbed through the hatch. She skipped past Comet and gave me a hug. "Wow, finally we get to meet in person." Then she turned to Comet and hugged him too. "Hi, Comet!"

A second later, her parents were through the hatch. Each shook our hands very formally. "How long until we can enter *Provider*?" Mr. Evolt asked, a little coldly I thought.

Comet checked his mTalk. "Five minutes."

"Five minutes too long, if you ask me," Mr. Evolt said.

"Safety first, Carl," Mr. Waves said.

The tension was palpable between the two men. I remembered that ASN had tried to send compatible families, but this relationship did not feel cordial at the moment. Maybe it was the journey. Spacefaring did that to people, especially if they'd been terrestrially bound for an extended amount of time prior to their journey.

"Yes, of course," Mr. Evolt droned. "Safety."

"I'll be happy to have access to my lab once again," Mrs. Evolt said. "I assume everything is set up for us," she added to no one in particular.

"Yes, your cabin is all arranged," Comet said. "My family saw to that personally."

"Good," Mrs. Evolt said.

No "thank you," I thought. *Just "good."*

"And my lab?"

"Well, that would be a question for Dr. Helios," Comet said.

"Helios?" she said. "Ha! I'll just speak to Commander Pujols if there is an issue."

I rolled my eyes.

Then Orbitus returned with several cases and satchels. He set them near the Waves family.

"Boys, you can retrieve our luggage," Mr. Evolt said, nodding toward Comet and me. "It's just in the corridor there."

Without looking, I knew Comet's face was as red as Mars. *The gall of these people.* But Comet didn't object. Instead, he waved at me to follow. We gathered the items in the hall—twice as many bags per person as the Waves family had.

"The remainder of the equipment and supplies will be offloaded over the next two days," Comet explained.

The light above the airlock hatch leading into *Provider* flashed green. KEWD spoke: "You are clear to enter. Welcome to *Provider.*"

Comet opened the hatch. "Gavin, please show the Waves family to their cabin, and I will take the Evolt family to theirs."

"Roger that," I said.

I heard a giggle behind me, and I turned to see Lilly. She waved, smiling broadly, but she stopped when her mom squeezed her arm. Mrs. Evolt's expression seemed to me to be as cold as the rock-ice of Titan's surface.

As we crossed through the hatch, Aurora stepped into view. Solar reached her in a flash and gave her a huge hug.

"It's so great to see you!" she said.

"You too," Aurora responded. "I can't wait to hang out with you here."

"Is there somewhere we can lounge and drink coffee?" Solar asked.

"No more coffee for you today," Mrs. Waves interjected with a laugh.

"Yes, Mom," Solar said.

"We can go to the galley, or we can sit next to the Titan Observation Port," Aurora said. Then she lowered her voice, "Or I know a great spot in the aquaponics greenhouse."

"Sounds great!" Solar giggled.

I led the Waves family to their cabin. Orbitus shoved past me without so much as a thanks. Then he dropped his luggage and plopped into one of the air loungers.

"Do you need anything else?" I asked.

"No, that should be it," Mr. Waves said.

"Thank you, Gavin and Aurora," Mrs. Waves added kindly.

"Yes, thank you," Mr. Waves added.

"Message me when you're ready," Aurora said to Solar.

"We will see you later," I said, and Aurora and I left. Comet was approaching from the direction of the Evolts' cabin. His expression was pure frustration.

"All settled and happy?" I asked.

"Settled, sure. Happy? For them . . . impossible," Comet said.

"It can't be all that bad," I said.

He shrugged. "Well, we did our job. The Evolt and Waves families have been greeted."

"Now what?" I asked.

"I'm going to check in with Dad and Mom, then I'm going back to the cabin," Comet said and stalked off to our hatch.

Aurora shrugged and then put a hand on my shoulder. "It's never easy meeting new people, and no matter the amount of personality or compatibility tests we take, some people just won't get along. But . . ."

And then I knew what was coming.

"I went outside to find a friend, but could not find one there. I went outside to be a friend, and friends were everywhere," Aurora said, repeating a favorite quote of our grandmother's. She'd said it to us ever since I can remember.

"Well, you and Solar really have hit it off," I said. "But I'm not sure anyone can befriend Orbitus."

Aurora's smile told me she thought differently.

"Lilly, on the other hand—she's quite friendly," I said. "And *nice*."

Aurora laughed. "Oh, brother. I do believe your cheeks are the color of Martian soil."

"Huh?"

Then Aurora's mTalk beeped. "It's Solar." Not even a second later, Solar's head popped into view, her braided black hair bouncing as she dashed down the corridor. She hugged Aurora again.

"I still can't believe we finally get to talk in person!" She grabbed my sister's arm. "You're *real*." Then she giggled again.

"To the jungle, then!" Aurora said. Before she disappeared around the corner, she shouted back, "They're *everywhere*, Gavin. Even in space."

I shrugged and headed toward the Waves family's cabin. *I could do this.*

"Gavin," Comet said, peeking out from our cabin. "They did it; Dad and Mom will be back by tomorrow morning. We're finally going to Inspire!"

"YES!" I shouted and ran back to our cabin.

IIIIIIIIIIFaiTH aT THe eDGe: GReeTinGs!

Welcoming new people into your life can be challenging, especially if those people get on your nerves. But Jesus never said that following God's commandment to "love your neighbor as yourself" would be easy. Jesus illustrated this point with the story of a Samaritan who had cared for a wounded Jew during a time in history when Samaritans and Jews were enemies. Jesus concluded with an admonition to be neighborly to anyone you happen to meet by showing kindness and mercy, which can mean being kind to someone who has wronged you or helping someone who needs it (Luke 10:25-37).

As Gavin's grandmother often said, being neighborly often means making the effort to reach out to someone else first. Many times, you'll be rewarded for that effort with a new friend.

Even if your neighborly gesture goes unreciprocated, take comfort in knowing that God counts whatever kindnesses you do for others as kindnesses done for Him, whether it's providing people with food, drinks, and clothing, visiting those in prison, or welcoming strangers.

Then the righteous will answer him, saying, "Lord, when did we see you hungry and feed you, or thirsty and give you drink? And when did we see you a stranger and welcome you, or naked and clothe you? And when did we see you sick or in prison and visit you?" And the King will answer them, "Truly, I say to you, as you did it to one of the least of these my brothers, you did it to me."

—MATTHEW 25:37-40

EXPLORATION ----------------------

1. Have you ever had to welcome strangers or new people to your home or school? How did it go? Looking back, what might you have done differently?

2. Read the parable of the Good Samaritan found in Luke 10:25-37. What are a few ways you could be a Good Samaritan to a neighbor this week by showing kindness and mercy to the people around you?

    "And so tomorrow, we officially board *Hopper* and head for Titan. After landing, our family will focus all our energy on assembling our living quarters." A smile curled Dad's lips. "You, my fellow explorers will join us there. Here is to a successful launch and the birth of a new settlement!" Dad raised his glass of sparkling water in a toast.

    Everyone cheered.

    Commander Pujols had organized a dinner for all three of the Inspire colonist families as well as the crews of *Provider* and *Beyond*. Tables had been pushed together, and Chef Raytza—using fresh supplies from *Beyond*—had made a gourmet meal unlike any she'd crafted thus far. Everyone was celebrating, and everyone was in high spirits. This is, after all, why *Provider* had been constructed, to support the Inspire settlement on Titan. A new home for humankind was the purpose of this entire endeavor, and here we were about to begin. Everything else had been preparation for this moment.

The three girls sat together at the end of our table, while Orbitus sat across from Comet and me. The parents and senior leadership of *Provider* were on the opposite end, while the other support crew of *Provider* and the *Beyond* crew took up the middle, talking space-life shop. The dinner had gone smoothly, everyone was getting along, and dessert had just been served.

"I can't wait to get down to Titan," Lilly said. "It's too bad we have to wait up here."

"We'll get there soon enough," said Solar, taking a bit of chocolate moon cake.

"Yes, soon enough to miss out on the work," Comet said.

Solar and Aurora both frowned.

"I'm joking," Comet said, but it seemed clear no one believed that.

"What's the first thing you're going to do on the surface?" Lilly asked. She was looking at me.

I swallowed and struggled to find my voice. "Uh . . . bounce."

Comet laughed.

I jabbed him with my elbow and restated, "I'm going to bound as far as I can across the surface."

"And you?" she asked Comet.

"I plan to climb to the nearby ridge—called *the Overlook*—and plant an ASN flag."

"Hasn't an ASN flag been planted already?" Orbitus teased.

"Yes," Comet said, "but this one will be at a higher elevation and easier to spot from the surrounding area. The rumor is that Galactic Prime will soon launch *their* first human-crewed ship to Titan. We need to establish which group was here first, before different companies start grabbing land to use."

"I read about Galactic Prime's launch," Solar said. "But I also read the destination wasn't announced yet. It could be headed to Mars or Luna."

"Too big for just going to Luna," Comet said. "It's a massive, interplanetary-sized ship."

Orbitus glared at Comet's retort. "Well, Titan isn't a planet, either."

Solar sighed. "Semantics. What will you do first, Aurora?"

Aurora grinned her bright smile. "I want to try to find one of the geysers," she said.

"Oh, I want to do that too!" Lilly said. "My dad said we will learn a lot about the subsurface oceans from those geysers."

"Your dad . . ." scoffed Orbitus under his breath, muttering something. Thankfully, Lilly didn't hear him.

But Comet did. "What's your problem?" he said to Orbitus.

Orbitus straightened. "*My* problem?"

"Relax, Comet," I said, putting my hand on his shoulder. Orbitus grinned at that, and Comet shifted under my hand. I was worried he was going to punch Orbitus or something.

"I wonder if we'd be the first family to live on Titan if my grand-parents were as wealthy as yours," Orbitus said directly to Aurora.

Aurora's eyes welled with tears almost immediately. It'd only been three years since our grandparents had passed. They'd died only hours apart.

Solar put her arm around Aurora, glaring back at Orbitus. "What's wrong with you tonight?"

Aurora cleared her throat, "I need to excuse myself for a moment." She stood and left the galley quickly. My mom must have noticed, because she stood to go after Aurora, but Solar was already following her and waved my mom off. "I got this," she said.

Comet turned on Orbitus. "What *is* your deal, man?"

I leaned forward and stared daggers at Orbitus, letting him know I agreed with the question.

"My deal is that you get to be one of the few families in all of humankind to step foot on a celestial body before anyone else *just* because your family has lots of money," Orbitus said.

Comet stood, his chair screeching backward across the floor. Now his face was purple-red with anger. The adults all stopped, and everyone stared in our direction.

I stood and put my arm around my brother. "Why don't you go ahead back to the cabin? I'll be right behind you."

Comet sighed deeply, and then sharply turned on his heels to head out of the room. The adults watched him leave. Commander Pujols's expression was quite serious. I gave everyone an "it's fine" smile. I pushed Comet's chair back in and took my seat again.

Lilly was still enjoying her chocolate moon cake, apparently uninterested in taking sides. Maybe she agreed with Orbitus's take on our family. Either way, I knew it wasn't true. If it were, I might feel like Orbitus, especially if our roles were reversed.

My grandparents never gave any money to ASN—their focus was on helping the less fortunate, those who were living in poverty. And while they agreed with my parents' decision to expand humankind's reach around the solar system, they believed that their calling from God was to help those on Earth however they could.

"Look Orbitus," I said. "My grandparents did well for themselves, yes, but my family never paid to get here or to be the first to the surface. You know that—you've been part of all the same mission planning meetings I've been in. You can ask anyone at ASN command. Neither of your parents ever applied to become commanders of this mission. Nor did they even want the job—they're both highly skilled specialists in their own rights. So it's not a question of money, it's a question of rank and role."

Orbitus still glared.

"We can't change the past, what our parents chose for themselves or for us," I said. "We can only make the best of the path we are on now. So I have a suggestion for you. Go find Aurora and apologize to her. She was very close to our grandparents, and your words really hurt. She would give almost anything to just talk with them again."

Orbitus stared daggers at me for a moment, but then his expression melted into something else. He nodded, and then he stood up.

"You're right," Orbitus said. "Would you go with me?"

"Sure thing," I said, and we started for the hatch.

"I'm coming too," Lilly said, chasing after us.

Behind me, I heard one of the adults say, "Isn't it nice to see them all getting along?"

If only they knew.

FaiTH aT THe eDGe: BULLYING

Knowing how to respond to conflict with a peer can be tricky. Do you stand and fight? Do you run? Do you try to ignore the problem? Does being a victim of bullying or being an onlooker change what you do? Each situation has unique circumstances that can require a unique response.

Sometimes it is necessary to stand up to a bully in order to prevent further injury. Solar, Comet, and Gavin weren't going to let Orbitus continue to hurt Aurora with his words.

But notice which response had the most powerful effect on Orbitus. Was it accusation and confrontation? Or was it understanding and explanation? In that tense moment in the galley, Gavin recognized a big truth: angry accusations just add more heat to the problem, but a gentle, levelheaded explanation has the power to cool the flames.

> A soft answer turns away wrath, but a harsh word stirs up anger.
> —PROVERBS 15:1

How did Gavin know what to say? Gavin paused and considered the situation from Orbitus's point of view. He was able to look past his own anger and understand *why* Orbitus might be acting the way he was. Gavin then gently spoke the simple truths that Orbitus needed to hear, without further provoking him.

EXPLORATION -

1. Have you ever had to deal with a bully? If so, what did you do? What happened? Did the way you responded help the situation?

2. Do you have a bully in your life right now? Why do you think that person might be acting that way? With that in mind, what might be the best way to respond to him or her? Ask God to help you know the truth!

3. Read 2 Corinthians 5:14-17. Here Paul talks about how Jesus' loving self-sacrifice gives Christians a new life, one with a less self-centered way of looking at the world and the people around us. How does being a "new creation" affect the way you interact with people every day at school and at home?

I stared out at the hazy surface of Titan as *Hopper* descended ever more closely to the surface, bringing Inspire into focus with every second of descent. This was really happening! I was about to step onto Titan. Mars had been my birthplace, but Titan would be my new home. I believed this was God's plan for my family—what the Evolts would have called their destiny. I'm not sure about the idea of having a destiny, but I know God has a plan and a design for our lives, and I wanted to follow His will wherever I lived.

Moments from now I would step out onto the Titan surface and be one of just five people ever to have done so.

"Landing gear locked," KEWD confirmed. "Retro rockets activating in three, two, one."

Hopper shook briefly as the retro rockets slowed our descent, bringing us into a soft touchdown.

"Landing successful," KEWD said. "System standby activated."

We broke into cheers, followed by a congratulatory message from Commander Pujols, who was following our progress from the command module aboard *Beyond.*

"Gavin, would you like to be the first to exit?" Dad asked.

I was surprised. "Really?"

"Absolutely," Dad said.

"Wait," Aurora interrupted. "Let me get a picture of this. Smile, Gav."

I didn't want to wait, but I did as asked.

"Are you ready?" Mom asked. I was. So I released my harness and stepped toward the hatch.

"Hatch lock deactivated," Dad said.

"Pressurization complete," Comet added.

"Okay, son, go ahead."

I took the handle and swept it up. There was a pop, and the hatch swung outward. I moved into the airlock space, then closed the hatch behind me. As the second hatch opened, I saw the Titan surface stretching out before me, a hazy, yellow-brown alien surface. None of the pictures or videos, no matter the quality or resolution, could ever have done it justice. This was my home now. *This is my future.*

I looked back and my mom gave me a thumbs-up, then I bounded through the hatch and down the ramp. I bounded forward across the surface, leaving *Hopper* behind me. White ice dust billowed behind me like a haze. The dust hung in the low gravity before slowly settling back to the ground.

"Gavin, you are the youngest person ever to step onto Titan," Aurora said.

"Duh," Comet said.

"In fact, you are the youngest to ever be part of a first group of space explorers," she added.

Comet didn't say anything; it was probably getting under his skin that I was now a record holder, a record unlikely to be broken anytime soon.

"Wait up," Aurora said. I looked back to see her bounding toward me. I was still gliding forward, nearing a rift in the ground. I'd studied all the terrain maps of Titan, but especially the area closest to Inspire. I stopped and Aurora stepped next to me.

"We did it," I said. "We're here!"

"I know! It's amazing!" she replied. "All of our training. All of our preparation."

"All our waiting," I added.

And then Comet was there, near us. He grinned at Aurora. "If Gavin is the youngest boy, then you're the youngest girl."

I saw Aurora's smile through her visor.

"Congrats to both of you," Comet said, his voice sincere.

We stood and stared out across the Titan landscape. It was beautiful in its own unique way. To know that God had created this celestial body so long ago and that humans had only now just reached it and could experience it for the first time. What other amazing places had God created but had yet to be explored by people?

"Kids," Mom called. "Come on back for a minute. We will have lots of time to explore, but first we want to do something."

"Race ya," Comet said, and we bounded back toward *Hopper*.

Comet was first back, and as Aurora stopped, she laughed. "Well, Comet, you officially hold the record of the first human to win a race on Titan."

Comet laughed heartily. "The reigning champion!"

"For now," I laughed.

"Kids," Dad began. "Gather closer." He held out a black book in his gloved hand. I recognized it; it was the family Bible passed down from Greystone to Greystone for more than two centuries. It'd been on two planets, and now two moons.

"Let's take a moment to thank and praise the One who not only allowed us to be here at this moment but kept us safe through this journey—who has been with us every moment," Dad said. "Let's bow our heads and thank our amazing God, the magnificent Creator of the universe."

We began to pray, each of us taking a turn to thank God for leading us to this place. Afterward, everyone was silent for a few moments as we looked at each other and all around us, allowing God's presence to settle over us.

"This Bible is a reminder of God's hand in our lives," my dad said. "For generations of Greystones, this book has been a source of truth and hope, of knowledge and comfort. We bring it here so that future Greystones will lean on God and not themselves. And for that we are thankful."

"Amen," we said in unison.

||||||||||FɑITH ɑT THE EDGE: THɑNKSGIVING

So much of Gavin's life has been building up to this moment—the moment when he first set foot on Titan. Although Gavin worked hard to make this moment happen, he couldn't have achieved it on his own. And while his family and ASN had their roles too, it was ultimately God who gave this moment to the Greystone family. God had made Titan in all its alien beauty.

God gave the ASN engineers the ability to develop technology that would enable human survival on the moon. He nudged Gavin's family along all the right steps—and that's just the beginning! It's beyond even an AI's mind to understand all the wonderful things God orchestrates and accomplishes. That's why the Greystones treasure their family Bible: it reminds them of the ways God has been working in their family for generations to bring them to this present moment. Today that remembrance filled them with a deep gratitude that they could only express by thanking God.

King David faced a similar moment in 1 Chronicles 17. God had taken him from being a lowly shepherd to being king of Israel. David wanted to do something to return the favor to God, but instead God lavished more blessings on David! All David could do was pray in awe before God as he thankfully reflected on who God is and all God had done for him.

> For you know your servant, LORD. For the sake of your servant and according to your will, you have done this great thing and made known all these great promises. There is no one like you, LORD, and there is no God but you, as we have heard with our own ears.
>
> —1 CHRONICLES 17:18-20, NIV

You may not be the youngest person to set foot on a moon, and you may not be the ruler of a nation, but God has worked in your life, and He will continue to do so.

EXPLORATION -----------------------

1. What have you done that would never have been possible without God?

2. Ask your parents or another adult relative how God has worked in your family's history.

3. Read Colossians 3:17 again. What words and deeds have you accomplished that would not be possible without God's guidance? Write down three things that God has done for you. Post this note in a place where you can see it.

S omething tugged my arm. "Gavin, wake up."

Blinking away a dream, I squinted at the body looming above my bed. "Dad?"

"Yes. Put on your TerraSuit. We're going for a ride in the rover. The rest of the family is waiting in the galley. Aurora saved you some Energen that you can grab on the way out."

Sleep forgotten, I sat straight up and rubbed fingers through my hair. "What's going on?"

"Something that won't happen again for another sixteen Earth days." Dad checked his mTalk. "Hurry! We leave in five minutes."

What special thing happens on Titan? I wondered. It's not like we'd discover new plant or animal life on a frozen moon. But before I could ask, Dad strode out the door.

Throwing off my thermal blanket, I scrambled after him. Goosebumps riddled my skin in the controlled air. We had lowered temperature during our artificial nighttime to help simulate a twenty-four-hour day. That cycle helped maintain our bodies' natural functions. After all, it's hard to get in sync with Titan on days that last for over two weeks.

After a quick change, we loaded both rovers—boys in one, girls in the other. Dad loaded destination coordinates and engaged KEWD's autopilot mode. Comet strapped in the back, monitoring the navigation map on a portable screen. I sat shotgun and scanned the front vid-screen showing a view of Titan's surface.

Not like I could see much. Because of its hazy golden-orange sky, Titan is already a dark world. Unlike Earth, only one percent of the sun's light reaches the surface. Thick, low-lying clouds give it a foggy appearance. It may be 300 times brighter than a full moon on Earth, but that's like a candle flickering in a vast underground cave.

Studying various shades of darkness soon got boring. "Are we there yet?" I asked.

Dad checked his mTalk again. "I told KEWD to stop the rover at a tall ridge I spotted on the map. We should arrive in five minutes. Just in time."

I narrowed my eyes. "In time for what?"

"A hike." Dad cleared his throat. "The rover won't go the full distance. We need to maintain our muscle mass anyway. The walk will do us good."

Precise as ever, our rover soon stopped. A rumbling sound prompted me to check the rearview vid-screen. Mom and Aurora had rolled up behind us.

After Dad lifted a pack onto his shoulder, he clipped a transmitter on the inside of my already snug helmet. "For later," he said as we disembarked. The new equipment emitted a faint laser beam across the bridge of my nose.

My helmet kept a continuous supply of oxygen flowing, and the thick atmosphere and low gravity on Titan's surface made movement a bit like swimming in water. But it was still hard to see.

"Phoenix." Mom switched on her headlight. "It's still pretty dark. We should pull out those EYE masks now."

"Eye masks?" I asked, turning on my own light. "Like those things you sleep in at night?"

"Eye masks," KEWD announced through the comms in our helmets, "can indeed refer to coverings placed over one's eyes to simulate darkness for the purpose of increasing one's quality of sleep. However, the letters EYE can also be an acronym for Electromagnetic Ytterium Masks. So 'eye masks' in this context means the Electromagnetic Ytterium Equipment masks."

"Yes, KEWD, thank you," Dad cleared his throat. Then he checked his mTalk again, nodded, and dropped the bag he carried to the ground. Opening the top, he pulled out five EYE masks rolled like scrolls and handed one to each of us.

Following Dad's lead, I flattened the flexible, membrane-like material. Dad, meanwhile, pressed the mask over the viewing

portion of his helmet and smoothed out the edges to stick it in place. Now I couldn't see his face at all!

"How does this help?" I held it away from me like a stinky sock.

"It's actually genius. I feel like I have cat vision." Dad swept an arm wide. "I can see everything out to the horizon."

Comet grunted. "But how does it work?" Comet seemed to dislike the idea of covering his eyes as much as I did.

Dad helped me put mine on.

KEWD spoke into our comms, "The human eye can only detect a small part of the electromagnetic spectrum. This equipment absorbs all that input and transmits through your faceplate to your eyes. That's why there is a receiver inserted in your helmet."

As soon as I engaged the EYE mask, the world around me came into sharp focus. Ice rocks bulged from the ground like giant blobs of potatoes. The foggy clouds now seemed like flashes of glitter. Ahead of me, the ground rose in a steep incline. There was some kind of hill up there.

Dad took the lead with the rest of us trailing behind. The resistance of the atmosphere against my suit reminded me of walking chest deep in our space training pool facility.

When we reached the top of the ridge, Dad paused. We crowded around him as he checked his mTalk. "Okay, we are just in time. Count down with me now. Five, four, three, two . . . one."

A beam of light broke through the darkness, newborn rays enhanced by the power of the EYE mask. I sucked in a breath and scanned the horizon. To my left, hydrocarbon grains and ice rocks were piled into sweeping dunes. To my right, a silvery methane river cut canyons through the ground and, beyond that, emptied into a lake with a tiny island dotting the center of it. Saturn, in all its massive glory, dominated the skyline. The raw and cold beauty of Titan overwhelmed me. I dropped to my knees.

"It's gorgeous," Aurora whispered, turning full circle with her arms wide.

"Wow," Mom murmured, nodding in agreement.

Comet cupped his helmet in his hands. "I've seen satellite images, but who could've imagined how awesome reality was?"

"God did." Dad crossed his arms across his chest. "It was His creativity that crafted the galaxy. His thoughts are higher than our thoughts, His ways beyond our understanding. And I wouldn't have it any other way."

Then Dad started singing: *Then sings my soul, my Savior God to thee. How great thou art. How great thou art.*

We all joined in the old hymn, our voices echoing over the speakers in the confines of our helmets, our hearts beating as one.

How great thou art.

IIIIIFAITH AT THE EDGE: TOGETHERNESS

Gavin and his family shared an amazing experience—the dawn of a new day on Titan. In that moment, they sensed a strong connection, a spirit of togetherness and harmony and fellowship. This sense of unity is part of the reason the Bible says, "Oh come, let us worship and bow down; let us kneel before the LORD, our Maker" (Psalm 95:6).

Sure, we can worship God on our own, but when we are surrounded by a community of friends, family, and other believers, that connection runs deeper. Togetherness means you've got people on your side rooting for you, people who understand what's going on in your heart because they're by your side experiencing the same thing.

Spending time with family is important. But with school and sports and music and clubs, our schedules can get so busy we forget to spend time simply being together with our family. You can encourage family togetherness by making time for joint meals, family devotions, and prayer. Ask your mom or dad to make a family game or movie night once a week. Make spending time together a priority.

EXPLORATION -----------------------

1. List three activities you've done together as a family. Highlight one of them and describe what you enjoyed about it.

2. Write down two obstacles you face that prevent you from doing things together with your family. How can you lessen the impact of those challenges?

3. List one special activity you think your family would enjoy doing together. What steps can you take to make it happen?

I slowly opened my eyes, my mind still groggy from sleep. KEWD hadn't even sent out a morning wake-up call yet, but something had woken me up. Feeling thirsty, I groped for the water bottle I always left on the table by my bed. I felt nothing but empty air. I sat up and conked my head on the ceiling above me. *What in the world?* As my brain clicked into gear again, I remembered it all. Titan. Inspire. Our hab-dome. We had made it! *Sleeping on the top bunk is going to take some getting used to,* I thought to myself as I rubbed my head.

I swung my legs over the side, carefully climbed down the ladder, stood, and stretched. I turned to go find some water, but a whimper stopped me. I glanced over at Aurora's bed across the room from mine and Comet's bunk beds. Even though Inspire's nighttime security lights are pretty dim, I could barely see my sister's outline. Aurora was sitting up in her bed. She had her head down on her knees, hugging them up to her chest. I heard a soft crying as I watched her gently rock herself back and forth.

"Aurora?" I asked as I padded over to her. "What's wrong?"

She didn't look up; her sniffling continued as she unclasped a hand from her knees and held up a finger, indicating for me to wait.

So I waited. I sat down next to her on the bed, draped my arm over her, and waited. Gradually her rocking slowed, and her sniffles became less frequent. Finally, she looked up at me.

"Thanks, Gavin," she said.

"Are you okay?" I asked.

"I'm fine. Or at least, I will be. This is just all so new. We were on *Provider* for five years."

"Yeah, this place is hard to get used to, isn't it?" I smiled grimly and rubbed my head. "But we'll make it."

"I know. I guess that's what happened to me. Everything just hit me all at once—I mean, yeah, we just moved from our old home and we're living in a newly constructed settlement on an unexplored moon, but it's more than that. Everything that we've been working toward for years—Gavin, we did it! We're here, the first humans on Titan! There's so much to do and see!" Aurora let out a soft squeal as she enthusiastically waved her arms.

Her excitement was contagious. I grinned in the dim light. "I can't wait!"

"Me, neither." She grinned back at me. Then her face softened as she added, "Thank you for sitting with me, Gavin. That means a lot."

I shrugged. "I didn't do anything."

"Yes, you did! You gave me time to think, and having you close by helped me process. That's all I needed."

"Glad I could be here," I said as Aurora reached over and gave me a hug.

IIIIIIFAITH AT THE EDGE: PRESENCE

Jesus said in John 15:13, "Greater love has no one than this, that someone lay down his life for his friends." Of course, Gavin didn't physically die for his sister today, but in a way he did lay down his life by temporarily putting his needs and plans on hold. He wanted to be present with her when she needed him.

It's easy to think of showing love as "doing" something for others. It's true; that is part of love. But notice that Gavin didn't really *do* much for Aurora. No fancy gifts. No big favors. No, he simply sat with her and waited with her. And then he listened when she was ready to talk. By doing this, he showed his love for his sister.

So, what is love? In 1 Corinthians 13, often called the "love chapter," the apostle Paul reveals that true love is an internal commitment—an attitude in your heart—that is expressed through outward actions. Whether those actions are big or small, it's the love behind them that matters.

Gavin had no capability to fix or solve what Aurora was feeling. Yet his small action of pausing his life to sit with her brought her comfort. Gavin's patience and presence demonstrated his love for his sister.

Love is patient and kind; love does not envy or boast; it is not arrogant or rude. It does not insist on its own way; it is not irritable or resentful; it does not rejoice at wrongdoing, but rejoices with the truth. Love bears all things, believes all things, hopes all things, endures all things.

—1 CORINTHIANS 13:4-7

EXPLORATION -

1. Have you ever sat with a family member or friend who was going through a hard time? How did they respond to your presence?

2. Have you ever been comforted by simply knowing someone you love is nearby?

3. Read the entire "love chapter"—1 Corinthians 13. Is there someone in your life who needs to recognize that they are truly loved? How can you demonstrate that you care for them?

R ecently I've been reading about early astronauts. What a different life they had in space! Did you know that early astronauts cleaned themselves with a towel, soap, and just a tiny bit of water because they didn't have the resources to conserve water? And without gravity, water and soap suds stick to everything. Later, they developed a tube-shaped shower. To use it, rocketeers had to strap themselves in so they wouldn't float off, hose themselves off, and suction every drop away with a vacuum. Ugh!

Luckily, Titan has natural gravity and Inspire is a high-tech facility. Our living quarters on this mission have had actual showers like you might find on Earth. True, we still have to recycle the water because our resources are limited. In fact, we even collect urine, which is about 95 percent water, and cycle it through a filtering system so the water can be used again.

I try not to think about that part too much. Especially when I'm brushing my teeth.

But that whole "limited resource" thing was why we kept our showers brief. At least, most of us tried.

"Comet, come on!" I pounded on the bathroom door. "It's my turn to shower next and you've been in there for fifteen minutes. What are you doing, washing every individual hair on your body?"

"Leave me alone. I'm not done yet!" he yelled back.

I slumped against the wall and counted the seconds. It took 300 beats until I heard suctioning, which meant Comet was finally cleaning up whatever dirt he'd left behind. Maybe the drippings would turn into Comet's coffee someday soon. A kid can dream, right?

"All yours." Comet opened the door.

The air temperature coming from the bathroom registered ten degrees warmer than the hallway, making me stand up straight. "It's about time," I said.

Comet slicked his hair back. "You're going to love this new setup. The water comes out instantly warm. So just step right in and enjoy."

"Thanks!"

Despite the added heat in the air, my skin goose-bumped as I stripped off my hab-suit. Holding my breath, I hopped into the shower as fast as possible, secured the cylinder-shaped shower wall, and yanked the lever to release the blissfully warm water.

Yow! Ice-cold water hit me full in the face instead.

"Ahhh!" I howled, shutting the flow off as fast as possible. I stood with my hand on the lever, dripping and shivering. The only heat in the shower came from my own body as my blood boiled. "COMET!"

Laughter echoed outside the door. "Sorry, Gavin. I must have used up all the hot water."

"You think?" I grabbed a towel and wrapped it around me. The fact that Comet heard me yell meant he knew there was only cold water left. He'd been waiting for my reaction.

I ground my teeth together. *And he'd told me to step right in.*

Still steaming with anger, I settled for one of those early astronaut cleanups. A towel, soap, and a touch of water. And all the while, I planned my revenge. So Comet wanted to use up all the hot water? If we were in a zero-gravity environment, I'd rig one of the toilets to malfunction. Then, when nature called Comet, he'd end up getting the mess all over himself.

Too bad that idea wouldn't work on Titan. Gravity, remember? Got to love it.

Maybe I could get a similar result though. I studied the toilet bowl. I knew how it worked. When sensors activated a flush, it opened a valve that sucked the contents out of the bowl and into a holding tank. Liquid was sent through a filter. Solids were stored in a tank that would later be burned. But what if the toilet didn't flush? Comet would be forced to clean out the toilet bowl by hand. And that . . . well, that would be perfect.

I studied the photo-sensor for a way to disable the auto-flush system. I could cover the "eye" with electric tape, but that would be too obvious. If Comet looked close enough, he'd spot it. I needed something clear that would still block the signal. Something invisible unless you knew it was there. Something like the silicone adhesive we used to fuse wires.

"That's it!" I dressed quickly and dashed to the mechanical room. A little rummaging around produced the silicone adhesive. I snuck back to the bathroom. Then I dabbed a bit of adhesive over the sensor. I stifled a laugh. Now, I just needed Comet to use the bathroom. Once he learned his lesson, I could come back and scrape off the evidence before anyone discovered my trick.

I found Comet in the galley finishing a breakfast shake. I grabbed a bottle of Energen and slid across from him at the table.

He smirked at me. "How was your shower, Gav?"

Frowning, I folded my arms across my chest. "It woke me up."

He laughed. "I bet. I would have paid to see your expression. No hard feelings?"

If he only knew. "No, it's fine. Sorry to get so mad. Here, you can drink my Energen."

Comet's eyes widened. "You love that stuff."

"I know." I shrugged. "But I'm not thirsty right now. Maybe if I share, you'll leave me a little hot water next time."

"Good thinking." Comet accepted my offering. "Man, drinking a breakfast shake and now this. I'm going to have to hit the lavatory!"

I smiled. *I'm counting on it.*

"Well, now *I* feel bad." Comet pushed a plate toward me. "This chocolate frosted donut is pretty rich. But it's so tasty, it's worth it. It's the last donut before we resupply. You want it?"

"Really?" I reached out and snagged the pastry. "Maybe you aren't so bad after all, bro. Thanks."

Taking small bites of the sweet treat, I watched Comet polish off his beverages. True, I hated to give up my favorite drink. But this donut made up for it. I licked a blob of chocolate frosting off my thumb, anticipating what would happen in Comet's bladder next, and how I would revel in my revenge.

Comet finally popped to his feet. "Well, I got to go!"

"To the bathroom?" I perked up.

He lowered his eyebrows. "No. I'm helping Dad in the science lab. And . . . well, I think I should apologize. It wasn't nice of me to take all the hot water. I won't do it again. But now we've got something to laugh about later, right?"

"Sure." I flattened my lips. "Plenty to laugh about."

"Okay." Comet threw his trash into the recycle bin. "Maybe I'll see you at lunch."

I waited until he left, listening hard in hopes that he'd have to make a mad dash for the lavatory. Instead, his footsteps echoed out of earshot down the hall.

And that's when the richness of my donut came knocking. *Toot.* I shifted in my seat and waved away a stinky odor.

"Oh, no." My stomach cramped. *Toot.* "This can't be happening."

I squirmed and pressed my hands into my stomach, trying to ease the pain of gas pushing against its inner lining. *I* needed the bathroom. *Toot.* I had time to clear off the adhesive and then reapply it. Right? *Too-oo-oot!* Forget the adhesive. I had to go. NOW!

Fighting off a wave of spasms, I sprinted down the hall and dove onto the toilet. I barely made it.

"Gavin, are you okay?" Comet yelled outside the door. "I saw you running."

"I'm fine. Just a little gassy." I groaned. "It was the donut."

"Sorry. I didn't warn you," Comet said. "Chef Raytza made it special. She probably experimented with a recipe. Guess I should have just thrown it out. But I hate to waste our resources, you know?"

"I know," I said.

"I'll leave you in peace. No more donuts though."

"Thanks, Comet."

Once again, his footsteps faded down the hall. And then I realized what I had done. And what I would have to do-do.

So much for revenge. I spent ten minutes holding my nose and scraping off the adhesive so the toilet would once again flush. My whole scheme had backfired.

Maybe I'd even tell Comet what happened. It would give us something to laugh about. Later.

||||||||||FaITH aT THE EDGE: REVENGE

Inspire is new, it's high tech, but its resources are limited. So when Comet deliberately used all the hot water for his shower, Gavin decided to get revenge on him. Of course, revenge doesn't always go as planned. Gavin rigs one of the toilets to not function properly but ends up having to use it himself.

In the Bible, God warns against taking revenge. Why would God caution us against this? Because when we seek vengeance, we are filled with *anger* instead of love. Our focus shifts to hatred, which is a negative emotion that eats us up from the inside.

Whenever we feel angry about the wrong done to us or to those we love, instead of striking back, we can take those feelings to God. He promises that He is the ultimate judge.

> Do not repay evil for evil or reviling for reviling, but on the contrary, bless, for to this you were called, that you may obtain a blessing.
>
> —1 PETER 3:9

EXPLORATION -----------------------

1. Describe a time when you felt hurt by someone and wanted revenge. What did you do?

2. Look up these verses about revenge. Write a five-word summary for each.
    - 1 Thessalonians 5:15
    - Leviticus 19:18
    - Mark 11:25

3. Regarding revenge, what pattern do you see in God's Word? What do you think is the hardest part about obeying these verses? How does God want us to deal with our desire for revenge?

"Your destination is on the right." KEWD's voice announced our arrival at a tall ridge, the one nearest to Inspire.

The rover rolled to a stop, and Dad checked our coordinates before shutting the motor off. "Ready to set up our new communications array, Gavin?"

"After all that simulator practice?" I hefted my Magnilox. "You bet!"

Dad laughed and unbuckled his safety strap. "Don't be too eager. We still have to haul the equipment to the top. Which makes me really glad advances in technology reduced the size of these subspace amplifiers." He gestured at the small network of transmitting and receiving antennae packed in the back of the rover. "Did you know the first communications array was actually a satellite thirty meters in diameter? It was called Echo—a passive spacecraft designed like a huge hot-air balloon."

"Whoa!" I tried to imagine the old relic. "We couldn't even have fit it in the rover."

"I know." Dad handed me a backpack filled with small antennae. "But at the time, the invention was cutting-edge. I bet the inventors could never have predicted how laser-based technology would make communication arrays compact, lightweight, and low-power. Or that even with Titan's thick atmosphere, we could still broadcast directly to Earth with an adapted millimeter-wave system."

I lifted a folded stack of the High-Efficiency Compact Surface Array Panels (HECSAP) as easily as grabbing a loaf of bread. I called them "hiccups" because if you read the letters really fast like a word, that's what it sounded like to me. "I bet they never imagined people would live on Titan either."

"True. But Titan obviously isn't perfect living conditions." Dad used his arm to guide me out the door and onto the surface. "That's why today's task is so important. The ability to communicate provides us and future Titan residents with a measure of safety. Should something happen to the *Provider*, we will still have a way to contact ASN on Earth."

I didn't like the idea of anything happening to the *Provider*—or of being stranded in space without a way to call for help. I shuttered. That would be just like every space-horror movie ever! "I never thought before about how important communication is."

"For humans, it's vital." Dad closed the hatch on the rover. "Without communication, how could we ever live in community, like God intended? How could we interact—like we are now? And how could we pass on information and knowledge?"

I shrugged. "There's always KEWD or video streams in the HUD to help you learn."

"I suppose." Dad shook his head. "But it's not quite the same thing, is it?"

I thought Comet and Orbitus could learn a thing or two about communicating. They were good at the talking part but not so much the listening part.

When we finally reached the top, the muscles in my legs burned from the exertion. I'd been so busy lately, I had skipped some of my treadmill sessions, and my body was paying the price.

"Tired?" Dad asked.

I stopped and took a few deep breaths. "This ridge is steeper than I thought."

"We need the added height to get a better broadcast. Don't worry, we only have a few more loads to transport." Dad patted me on the back. "It's worth the effort though. Communication is probably one of the most important skills we have, especially in space."

I thought about our family trip a few days ago when we used our EYE masks. I remembered how beautiful and big Titan looked but how overwhelmingly empty and silent it felt too. Having my family beside me sharing the experience and then talking about it later made that morning meaningful. Which made me wonder something else. "Is prayer like an even more advanced form of communication? Something better than lasers traveling on millimeter waves?"

Dad lowered his pack and pulled out his tools. "I suppose so. Prayer is an instant, direct line to God's throne. And we don't need any fancy equipment to contact Him either."

"What if something goes wrong?" I planted several "hiccups"

and adjusted the angles. "I mean, we could be in a lot of trouble if we can't communicate with the *Provider*."

"True. But even when we don't pray, God still knows what's going on." Dad pulled up his mTab. "Psalm 139 says, 'O LORD, you have searched me and known me! You know when I sit down and when I rise up; you discern my thoughts from afar. You search out my path and my lying down and are acquainted with all my ways. Even before a word is on my tongue, behold, O LORD, you know it altogether.'"

"Wait." I held up a hand. "If God knows all that, then why do we need to pray?"

Dad snapped an antenna in place and connected it to my panel. "Think of it this way: Without you saying anything to me, I can anticipate when you're hungry. Or when you're nervous. Or excited. Or when you want something. You don't have to tell me. But when you do talk to me about how you're feeling, we connect. And how I respond helps you understand me, too. Through that give and take, talking and listening, we develop a relationship."

"Oh." Chewing on my lip, I inserted another row of "hiccups" for Dad to program. "I like that idea. I think we should pray now!"

"You bet." Dad laughed. "But don't think that gets you out of two more trips up and down the ridge hauling more equipment. Am I communicating well?"

Smiling, I stood and stretched my aching legs. "Crystal clear, sir," I said.

IIIIIFAITH AT THE EDGE: COMMUNICATION

When Gavin and his dad erected a communication array, they discussed how important it was to interact with each other while they worked together. It's through talking and listening to each other that we learn new skills, express our feelings, and share ideas. Communication allows us to understand other people and allows them to understand us. That's why prayer and reading our Bibles is such an important part of the Christian life. When we pray, we can tell God our fears, our sorrow, and our dreams. We can ask for guidance and wisdom. We can ask for help in difficult situations.

God speaks to us, too, through His Word. Psalm 119:105 tells us that God's Word is like a lamp, lighting the path we should take. Within the books of Scripture, we can also find passages that encourage and comfort us or challenge our faith to grow in exciting new ways. All these things provide us with direction—a light on our path that helps us navigate this world's challenges.

> And your ears shall hear a word behind you, saying, "This is the way, walk in it," when you turn to the right or when you turn to the left.
> —ISAIAH 30:21

With all the busyness of life, it can be easy to skip prayer or time reading your Bible. You fix that problem by creating time, by wisely prioritizing the things that are important. Set your alarm twenty minutes early, keep a list of prayer requests, and make it a goal to memorize Scriptures that nurture your faith. These tasks will help you and God communicate.

EXPLORATION -

1. Create a list of prayer requests. Set aside the first ten min-
    utes of your day to pray about each item on your list.

2. Spend ten more minutes reading your Bible. As the weeks
    pass by, look for the ways God has responded to your prayers.

3. List three obstacles that might prevent you from continuing
    this practice of prayer and reading next week. Highlight the
    biggest one—the one that takes up the most of your time.
    Make a plan to combat this issue.

"**G**ood morning, all you people living on Earth, along with my fellow space-faring explorers." I flashed my biggest smile. "This is your host, Galactic Gavin here, builder of the stellar new communication array we're testing out, with the latest rundown on the galaxy's greatest graphic novels: *Cosmic Corsairs*." I pointed behind me. "Last episode, Captain Darkstone had detected our hero Beckett Blastoff hiding in the asteroid belt, and he was closing in for the—"

"Oh, no, no, no." Mom's image invaded my mirror. "You were instructed to wash up for the broadcast, not use your comb as a microphone to entertain yourself. And look at you." She stepped beside me and smoothed down a fold in my sleeve. "You've still got bedhead hair. No indication of teeth brushing going on." She pointed. "And I'm pretty sure that's a stain on your uniform."

I looked down and covered the spot with a towel. "You didn't complain about how I dressed yesterday."

"Yesterday you were hauling supplies, repairing constructo-bots, and scraping ice rocks off your boots." Mom placed a hand on both of my shoulders and turned me around. I could tell she had cleaned up for our presentation. The gold accessory belt around her waist shone. Her bodysuit's purple neoprene-coated nylon had a fresh glow. I bet she'd even polished the aluminized mylar lining on the inside!

Grunting, I sniffed my armpit. Not too bad.

"Today, we stream live in front of billions of people in—how soon, KEWD?"

"Fifty-two minutes and thirty-seven seconds," the AI responded.

"Right." Mom studied me with her hands on her hips. "And I don't want you looking like you just wrestled a solar flare and lost. Wash up, change into a clean uniform—that includes under-wear, Galactic Gavin—and for the sake of all Creation, brush your teeth. You've got to put your best foot forward."

"Why? You and Dad are doing most of the talking." I ran my finger over the comb, making the teeth twang. "All I have to do is introduce myself and then stand in the background and wave. No one will notice a little spot on my collar."

"I'll notice. And if I do, someone else might too. It's best to be prepared. Every broadcast is an opportunity to share what our world is like to people who have no idea what's in store for them if they come to Titan." Mom straightened her shoulders and stood tall. "That means when you step in front of that camera, you're not just Gavin Greystone. You're an ambassador for ASN reaching out to anyone wanting to explore space."

"Ambassador." Frowning, I pulled out of her grasp. "Doesn't that give me diplomatic immunity from grime crimes?"

"Ha ha, nice try." Mom handed me a washcloth. "Being an ambassador actually gives you *more* responsibility. When people see you, they associate you with ASN. What you say, how you dress, how you behave—these things should all reflect what ASN stands for. Unity. Community. Innovation. Bravery. A can-do spirit of adventure. And more importantly, hope for a better life." She folded her arms across her chest. "Your job is to show the best Titan has to offer. So ask yourself this: 'Am I a good ambassador, drawing people toward Titan, or a bad one, pushing them away?' What will the world see?"

Lifting my gaze, I checked the mirror. My cheeks heated, and I cleared my throat. "Got any more washcloths?"

An hour later, when the overhead lights blazed on and the broadcast went live, my dress uniform was crisp and clean and every hair on my head was in place. I looked pretty good. Which was especially important since then Dad threw me a curveball. After his speech, he opened the floor for questions. The ASN announced they had five, all submitted by elementary school children. And do you know what my dad did?

He smiled, passed me the microphone, and said, "Ambassador Gavin, I think you're the best qualified to respond to this one."

The first clip played; it was a little girl wearing a homemade ASN costume. "If you had a nickname, what would it be?"

My mom smirked and nodded to me.

"Galactic Gavin, of course!" I said.

I have to admit, Mom was right. Guess it pays to be prepared. You never know when you'll be the one people turn to for answers.

You never know when the spotlight will shine brightest on you.

//////FaITH aT THe eDGe: amBassaDOR

As leaders in space expansion, Gavin and his family repre-
sented ASN, making them ambassadors for the alliance. An
ambassador is a representative for something big and important. So ambassadors have many roles. They maintain a good
working relationship with other people. They serve as model
citizens, showing the rest of the world the mission and goals
of their company or country. Ambassadors are strong leaders,
peacemakers, and messengers. Everything—from how ambassadors
speak, carry out their business, and dress—reflects on whom
they represent. Even though Gavin might only briefly appear on
the screen, his mom recognized the impact that this appearance
might have on the viewers.

The Bible highlights the role of an ambassador too:

> Therefore, we are ambassadors for Christ, God making his
> appeal through us. We implore you on behalf of Christ, be
> reconciled to God.
>
> —2 CORINTHIANS 5:20

Let's unpack that a little bit. *We are ambassadors for Christ*
means that we might be the only example of a Christian someone
might ever see. *God making his appeal through us* means that our
actions will either draw others to Christ or push them away. Either
way, God uses us to reach others. *We implore you on behalf of
Christ, be reconciled to God* means that we should do our very best
to make sure we show others the best God has to offer. Treat others
the way Christ treats you. With kindness. Patience. Love. And joy.

What others know about God often comes from watching you—Christ's ambassador.

EXPLORATION -----------------------

1. List three people you interact with each day who need to know Christ. Highlight one person to pray for this week. In what ways can you be Christ's ambassador to that person?

2. Gavin prepared for the broadcast. You can be prepared with answers for someone who has questions about what you believe and why. How can you develop some clear answers? If you're stuck for ideas, read these verses in order to help guide you: Romans 3:23, Romans 5:12, Romans 6:23, Romans 5:8, Romans 10:9-10, and Romans 10:13.

T itan is an icy fortress of doom when Comet is in command
of the rover.

I gripped the armrest on my chair when another patch of ice
rocks appeared in the vid-screen, and I shot Comet a glare. "You're
driving around that this time, right?"

"Relax," Comet said. "I got this."

Three jarring bounces and a shot of whiplash later, I let out a
hiss of breath.

"Woo-ha!" Comet yelled, twisting the vehicle to the left.
"There's another pinball pit!" That's what he called areas dotted
with ice rocks—named after an old-fashioned game on Earth.

I tightened my grip.

Mom had said this mission would help Comet and me bond. Dad said it was an opportunity to develop our independence and skills. But what it felt like was riding in a blender.

"No more detours," I said. Bracing myself, I enlarged the navigation map. *How much farther was it?* "Tell KEWD to autopilot again."

"Oh, come on." Comet smirked. "You know that was fun."

"Sure, right, fun." I rubbed the back of my neck. "If fun means being terrified that your older brother is going to crash on a moon at the edge of the solar system and leave you with nothing but a headache!"

"No, I'd leave you with a comet wrapped in bacon. A meateor!" Comet laughed—a contagious kind of belly-jiggling barking that got me snickering too.

"Well, I wouldn't be hungry," I said. "Because, well, I've already had my . . . *launch!*"

"Good one." Comet flipped a thumbs-up. "You're a star."

"Aw, quit mooning," I quipped.

"Woo-hoo!" Comet doubled over. "We've got to stop cracking jokes, or I'll pop a seam."

"Why?" I sat up straighter. "I mean, it's not like we . . . *planet.*"

Funny how tension melts out of your body when you smile. And so let's just say I was more relaxed by the time KEWD announced we'd arrived at the cryovolcano.

As we rolled to a stop, a rhythmic patter hit the outside of the rover. "What's that?" I asked.

Comet pointed at the vid-screen. A plume of vapor dissolved like steam in the air. "Those would be fine, frozen flecks of a mixture of water and methane raining down." The grin on Comet's face widened. "The cryovolcano must have just erupted."

My heart kicked into high gear. I matched his smile. "Like snow?"

Comet unbuckled. "Want to find out?"

I stared at the vid-screen for a moment. Infrared filters picked up glitters of light. Ice flakes, not snowflakes. Or so I guessed from our videos I'd seen. "Yes!"

Comet popped his door open first, but I scrambled out of the rover before he did. I've read about how snow on Earth falls at a steady rate from the skies, but the fallout from the cryovolcano lasted barely as long as the outburst. Now only a handful of ice particles littering the ground hinted at the eruption. "I guess we missed it," I said.

"We'll be here for a while setting up this sampling station. Maybe it will blast again." Comet turned around. "Help me unload the equipment."

For the next hour, Comet and I worked and joked around as we deployed a spindle-legged robot we nicknamed Spidey. That's what it looked like—one of the large spiders that Dr. Sprucevine kept alive in the astrobotany lab.

The goal was for Spidey to crawl up to the edge of the cryovolcano and launch our first Deployable Underground Gadget (DUG), an autonomous probe shaped like a torpedo that burrowed through the ice. The way Ms. Carver, *Provider*'s chief engineer, described it, DUG relied on a tiny nuclear reactor to power a drill head that buzz-sawed through layers of ice. The onboard reactor worked sort of like a thermos that keeps your soup warm all day, but this container holds deuterium and tritium instead of chicken and noodles. DUG used special sensors to guide it and transmit data throughout its journey. When it reached the depth Dad had pro-grammed it to travel, DUG would suck in several samples. After that, the probe would melt the ice surrounding it, change direction, and drill its way back to the top. The whole process would take several hours.

After we made the final adjustments to the sampling station, Comet high-fived me. "I'm proud of us. We drove here by ourselves and assembled the equipment without any help. We tightened a few wires," he said, grinning. "And loosened a few screws."

"And now . . ." Grinning, I used the controls to guide our spindly-legged robot up the side of the cryovolcano, then punched in the codes that launched DUG on its journey below the ice-rock.

"There it goes," Comet said, as the machine cut through its first layer of ice.

"Too bad Dr. Helios isn't here to see this." I leaned forward to record a video to send him later. "He'd probably invent a holiday to celebrate."

We watched DUG at work until the tail end of it disappeared under the surface. Even though my TerraSuit protected me from the cold, I still shuffled in place, as if chilled. Fine grains of hydrocarbon, stuck together like packing peanuts, crunched beneath my boots.

"There's a lot here Dr. Helios would love. Like these dunes," Comet said.

I lifted my gaze. I'd never been on Earth to experience its sand dunes, but I'd heard they had the same windswept pyramidal shape as Titan's dunes. "I can't wait to see what DUG digs up. It's hard to believe there's actually an ocean of water under there."

"It's hard to believe the surface has lakes and rivers of liquid methane." Comet swept his arm outward. "Or actual mountains. They're named after mountains in *The Lord of the Rings*."

"Angmar Mons, Erebor Mons, Moria Mons," I recited, ticking off a finger for each. "Think we'll find a frozen hobbit here?"

Comet laughed and clapped a hand on my shoulder. "Let's double check to see if the sensors are online."

We'd only taken two steps when the ground trembled underneath us. I glanced over my shoulder, puzzled. Had DUG struck something?

"Look!" Comet pointed.

A shot of silver burst into the air, then billowed like a white firecracker. Almost instantly, the cloud vanished. Tiny crystals spilled over us.

I sucked in a breath. "The cryovolcano!"

"No way!" Comet pumped his fist. "We got to see an eruption after all! Who knows what we'll discover next?"

"We could see what it's like to ski down the side of a dune."

Comet stood stock still. "How much time do we have again?"

"Six hours—"

"Five hours, fifty-three minutes, and two seconds," KEWD corrected over my mTalk.

I pressed my lips together. "Give or take."

Comet craned his head as if checking out the nearest slope. "We'd have to protect the TerraSuits from tearing."

"We have the tools to remove the nameplate off the rover. We could use it like a sled."

"Ha!" Comet pulled me into a headlock, a sure sign of his excitement. "You're on. Race you to the rover." Pushing me away, Comet took off.

Smiling, I trailed behind him, taking my time. After all, Comet was in for another discovery. He might beat me to the rover. But I had the Magnilox tool we needed.

|||||||||||Faith aT THe eDGe: DISCOVeRY

As Gavin and Comet continued their mission, a kind of camaraderie, a companionship, formed between them. Not only did they have these moments of unity and friendship, but they learned new skills together and were able to explore more of Titan's surface. They even sledded down the dunes! But just like DUG took a small specimen of the massive ocean hidden underneath Titan's surface, Gavin only experienced a small sample of the vast mysteries of our awe-inspiring universe.

The Bible recognizes the incredible complexity of our world and points out that no matter how many wonders we discover, there are still more just beyond the horizon.

> Can you find out the deep things of God? Can you find out the limit of the Almighty?
> —JOB 11:7

Think about that. No matter how many planets and moons we study, how far we dive into our oceans, or how close we travel to the sun, God made it all. We cannot see the limits, even with our most sophisticated technology.

Creation reveals that God is eternal and powerful. In comparison, we are small. Even so, God still cares about every person. Their thoughts. Their victories. Their defeats. He cares about you—loves you so much that He even knows the number of hairs on your head! (Luke 12:7). He invites you to talk to Him and follow His ways. To be His child. And having a relationship with the Creator of the universe? Well, that might be the most astonishing discovery of all.

EXPLORATION -----------------------

1. Spend some time researching some of God's incredible creatures. The mimic octopus, blue glaucus, and mantis shrimp are all uniquely equipped to function in their environments. Pick one creature and write down some of the amazing and interesting things you discover about it.

2. Discover more about God with two action steps. First, claim and reflect upon one of God's promises found in Scripture. Then pray, asking God for wisdom and guidance as you learn to trust Him to keep His promises. You can select your own promise and prayers or use the following outline:
   - Promises in the Bible: Jeremiah 29:11 and Isaiah 41:10
   - What are the promises?
   - Prayer: God, thank you for _____. Please remind me to remember this promise when I need to better trust in You.

"**S**low down!" Comet shouted, leaning into me.

"No way." I flipped on the boosters and blasted past the first space station.

Clunk. Something landed on the table next to me. It clacked loud enough to make me jerk, which sent my cruiser crashing into an asteroid.

My screen showed a colossal explosion, and Comet yelled, "Ha! I win again."

"Dad!" Wincing, I dropped my mTab on my lap and slumped. "We were in the middle of an interstellar race. You distracted me. I could have won."

"You wish," Comet said. "You up for another go?"

"Boys!" Dad pointed at the broken drill bit he'd dropped. "Your break is over. I need a replacement drill for the CB-65's end-of-arm tooling, and we don't have extra parts here. Plus a few western slope solar units are experiencing issues, and I need to take a unit back to *Provider* for Ms. Carver to have a look at. Time for another supply run. And you know what that means?"

I sat straight up. "A trip to *Provider*."

"Yep." Dad picked up the bit and pinched it between his fingers. "And since I need to collaborate with Commander Pujols during the journey, I need a pilot."

If I went with Dad, maybe Chef Raytza would fix my favorite dessert or Dr. Helios would show me improvements he made on his latest inventions. Even better, I would get to see Lilly Evolt again. Imagine how much she would laugh when I told her about Comet and the shower disaster! Best of all, I could fly *Hopper*. "I'll go," I said faster than a laser beam.

"No, I should go," Comet said. "You just pulverized your cruiser!"

I lifted my mTab and shook it. "Not the same."

Dad's lips flattened. "Much as I would enjoy letting you fly, Gavin, I want Comet to lead this trip."

Fire shot through my veins. "Why do you always choose Comet? Just because I'm younger doesn't mean I can't do anything. I pay attention. I know how to start *Hopper*, how to reverse boosters, and . . . well, how hard can landing and docking be anyway? You can always engage KEWD's autopilot."

"True." Dad put his hand on my shoulder. "But Comet has logged over 1,000 practice hours, so he's better qualified than you. In the case of a what-if, that kind of training matters."

"A what-if?" I asked.

"What if you have to switch to manual control to land?" Comet counted off on his fingers. "What if one of the hundreds of sensor alarms goes off? What if the forward thrust fails? What if the StarNav goes offline? What if the boosters misfire? What if there's too much pressure in the external fuel tanks? What if visibility is blocked? What if the touchscreen reboots in the middle of a maneuver? What if the safety hatches jam? What if—?"

"Okay, I get it." I folded my arms across my chest. I didn't understand how to solve half of the problems Comet just rattled off, but I didn't want him to know that. "I'll stay here and . . ." I waved my arm at the boring gray wall. "Count the power outlets."

Maybe Dad sensed how upset I was, because he dismissed Comet with a nod of his head. "Suit up. We leave in twenty minutes."

"Yes, Sir." Comet saluted, smiling bigger than I'd seen all week. I could hardly blame him.

Unable to meet Dad's gaze, I lowered my head and powered off my mTab. "I'll check on Mom," I said, turning to leave. "Maybe *she* wants my help."

"Gavin." Dad's voice compelled me to stop. "You're growing quickly and you have so many skills, I know you'll be a great asset on future missions. In fact, I look forward to the day when you're the one I enlist. But until then, remember this. Just because you want to do something doesn't mean you're equipped to do it, any more than telling Comet you're going to beat him in a race means you're automatically going to win."

"But being a pilot?" I threw up my hands. "That's a dream job."

"Anyone can dream," Dad said. "But it's the work you put into following a dream that makes it become reality. How much time have you devoted to training on the simulator?"

"I don't know." I shrugged. "A hundred hours?"

Dad snorted, as if trying not to laugh. "Try about a hundred minutes. You learned enough to start the vehicle and the basic rudimentary knowledge of flying. That's not enough expertise to safely execute the maneuvers needed for this operation. That's like tuning in a broadcast about coping with gravitational shifts but muting the sound and then trying to calibrate the correct centripetal force needed to stabilize the habitat based on the fact that you downloaded the podcast. You'll end up with zero gravity because you don't have the skills you need to operate the system. In that situation, can you imagine what might happen if Comet had an untimely burp?"

I laughed. A burp without gravity makes barf floating through the air. "We'd have Comet Vomit."

"Right. Now apply that same logic to today's excursion. What might happen if something unexpected happens on *Hopper*?"

"Something worse than vomit." I frowned. "Guess I'll never get to fly."

Dad ruffled my hair. "Not true. I absolutely want you to pilot for me sometime. After you've trained like Comet has for this type of mission. If you really want to pilot *Hopper*, then you should devote some of your free time to mastering navigation, memorizing the instruction manual, and learning the layout of *Hopper*'s cockpit controls. Do you understand?"

"Yes." My anger evaporated like exposed rocket fuel. Dad was right. I still had a lot to learn, but I hadn't developed a plan to learn it. Honestly, I had plenty of chances to listen to protocol and sit through simulated flying lessons. But while Comet put in the work to earn his wings, I tinkered with my Magnilox or played video games on my mTab instead. Even though age gave Comet a head start, I couldn't excuse my lack of effort.

"Hey, Dad!" Comet poked his head into the room. "Ready to go?"

Dad glanced at me, as if checking to see if I was okay with him leaving, so I answered for him. "Dad's ready. And I will be too."

"Really?" Comet lifted his eyebrows.

"Yep." I grinned. "In a few months. When I'm done training."

Comet cocked his head. "That seems pretty ambitious."

"No." I shook my head. "Because I already know how to make something fly. Time."

||||||||||| FAITH AT THE EDGE: TRAINING

Although Gavin was upset that Comet got to pilot *Hopper* instead of him, he soon realized the reason why his dad didn't pick him: he just wasn't prepared. He had not made time to properly train for all the what-ifs that could happen. Keep in mind, Gavin had the time and opportunity to prepare, but he let other things—like his video games and Magnilox—distract him from the work.

The Bible talks about training too.

> All Scripture is breathed out by God and profitable for teaching, for reproof, for correction, and for training in righteousness, that the man of God may be complete, equipped for every good work.
>
> —2 TIMOTHY 3:16-17

If we practice being kind, helping others, sharing the gospel, and obeying our parents on a daily basis, such actions will come automatically. But such discipline doesn't come without effort. Studying and memorizing Scripture can help you have a fast answer for people with questions about what you believe. It also serves as a guide for how you should behave. Prayer gives you an opportunity to talk to God and listen for His guidance. And being a good friend gives you a chance to practice kindness.

When we are put into stressful life situations, when we are tempted to do something wrong, when we are faced with failure, it is our faith and our training that will help us make it through.

EXPLORATION -

1. List three skills you would like to learn. Pick your favorite, and come up with a daily training plan.

2. Train yourself with God's Word. Pick one of these verses: Proverbs 3:5, John 14:6, Psalm 119:105, 2 Timothy 1:7, Galatians 5:22-23, or James 1:22. Write it down somewhere where you'll see it and memorize it this week.

3. What does it mean to be "equipped" for the good work God has in store for you (see 2 Timothy 3:17)? What steps can you take today to be adequately prepared for that work?

"**A**nd this is just for fun." I twisted my hands hard to the right, sending my digital *Hopper* into a sharp spin. My spaceship flashed through the virtual world like a rollercoaster gone rogue. If only Dad could see these moves!

The simulator's graphics and motion were so real that I fought off a wave of lightheadedness as the extreme g-forces hit me. Time to land. I straightened my virtual *Hopper's* trajectory into a smooth glide into base.

"Mission accomplished," I said, stretching my arms. A vidscreen displaying stats for training level eight replaced the digital replica of *Hopper's* control panel.

Dad and Comet wouldn't return to Inspire for at least six

more hours. Mom and Aurora were still out repairing an offline mining-bot. The itch to dive into the next level of training competed with the rumble of my stomach. I guess I could stop for food.

But all thoughts of eating vaporized as soon as I removed the headgear that helped produce the virtual reality magic. Red lights flashed. "Meteorites detected. Impact in two minutes. Take cover immediately," KEWD said.

What?

My vision spun like it had in the simulator. Everything had been fine when I started the program, so I'd turned off my comms. I mean, what could really happen in thirty minutes? But I'd gotten so into my training—I'd done eight sessions in a row without a break—that I'd been out of touch for the last four hours.

And I had missed the early warning system.

As I slapped on my mTalk, panic threatened to swallow me. There were twenty messages from Dad. I played the most recent one. "Gavin, I think the meteorites are interfering with our communication. I hope you're already locked in the storm shelter." His voice sounded clipped. "KEWD projects the biggest rock will strike nearby but miss the main building. We're praying for you."

Storm shelter? The thick-walled room in the center of Inspire never seemed further away. I sprinted down the hall, trying to remember my emergency training. The floor underneath me vibrated, making me stumble. I'd read that meteorites give off low frequency radio waves that can cause these tremors.

On Earth, you see lightning before you hear thunder, and you can use the seconds in between to calculate how far away the strike is. Any similar math wasn't going to be very helpful here though. This thing was just too *close*.

"Meteorites detected. Impact in fifty-nine seconds. Take cover immediately," KEWD warned.

I yanked open the storm shelter's heavy, titanium-plated door. My fingers shook so much, I mistyped the lock code twice before I remembered to use voice activation. "KEWD, seal shelter!"

"Meteorites detected. Impact in—" The rest of KEWD's message was lost in a sonic boom.

I clapped my hands over my ears as the shelter door hissed shut.

For six shaky breaths, I stayed curled up on the floor. Once my heart stopped trying to jump out of my chest, I opened my eyes. Everything was dark except the glow from my mTalk. Scrambling, I patted my arms, legs, face. All my body parts were still attached. I checked the status panel beside the shelter door. Life-support systems were running. It seemed safe enough to leave the shelter.

Dreading what I might find, I pushed open the shelter door. Darkness greeted me, but I could still see the outline of chairs, cabinets, and other hab-dome equipment. A moment later, machinery began to hum, whirr, and click back to life. Inspire's dim emergency lights and life support systems came on. The meteorites must have hit something that forced Inspire to use backup power.

My mTalk pulsed, and I checked the display. "Dad!"

"Gavin! Thank God I got through to you. Are you okay?"

"Yes, Dad, I am for now," I said. "Are you?"

"*Hopper* was struck by one of the meteorites, as was the primary solar array for *Provider*. It's all fixable, but the engineering team has to focus on the solar arrays before they can take a look at *Hopper*," he explained.

I knew what that meant; it meant it'd be a while before they returned to Titan.

Dad continued, "Our tracking shows a meteorite took out

reactor three, and all the electrical systems are offline. Can you confirm that Inspire shifted into backup power?"

"Yes, it did; lights are emergency, but KEWD shows life support system functioning," I explained.

"Good. Listen, Gavin, it's essential you get the power grid back online," Dad said. "Relying only on the backup generator isn't a scenario I want to be in for very long. If it failed, things might get . . . interesting."

You mean deadly. If anything happened to the backup power, I'd be relying on oxygen canisters until I could be extracted.

"That's not going to happen though, right?" I said.

The lights flickered. The line went quiet. "Right?" I repeated.

"Gavin, you're trained for all sorts of scenarios." Dad's voice faded, then came back. "God was looking out for us when we left you at Inspire. If you had come with us, no one would be close enough to get Inspire functioning again."

The lights faltered again, then dimmed. An uneasy prickle climbed down my spine. "Close enough? For what?"

Dad sighed. "To manually reset the reactors."

The hair lifted on my neck. I knew the layout of Inspire. I knew where the reactors were. The only way to do a manual reset was to put on a TerraSuit and exit the safety of the hab-dome. Who designed this place anyway, a mad scientist?

Remembering my earlier disaster trying to switch our equipment from auto to manual, I wiped clammy hands on my pants. Images of the settlement floating off into space like broken pieces of the Death Star flooded my mind. Normally, I'm all over the whole adventure thing. But with so much on the line? No way I wanted to be our only hope. "Can't it wait until you're back? Or what about Mom? She's close."

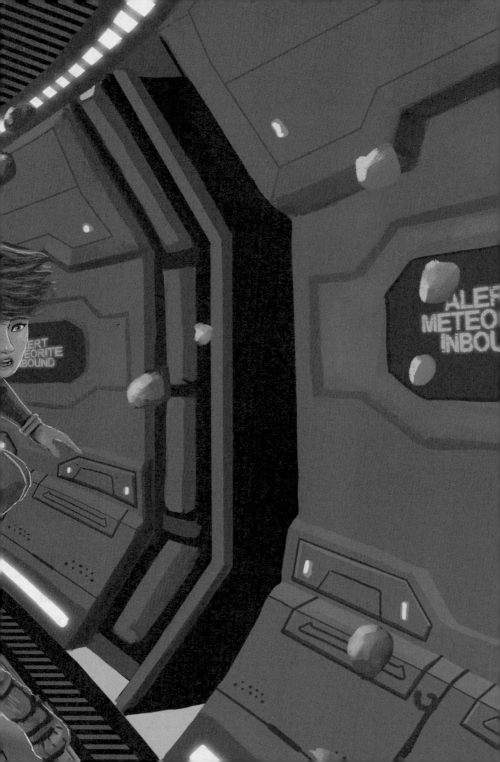

"No. I'm sorry, Gavin. The grid is crashing," Dad said. "I can't make it back in time. And I can't get in touch with your mother's rover."

My stomach kicked back like a rocket booster blasting off the ship. "But I . . . I've never trained for this. There was always a second-in-command or squadron leader or some other highly qualified person in charge of stuff like this. What if I mess up? What if my TerraSuit gets snagged and tears? What if—"

"You're scared. I know. I would be too."

Dad's words choked off my rant. It was difficult to imagine Titan Mission Commander Phoenix ever being afraid. I took a breath to steady myself. It didn't work. "I'm not sure I can do this, Dad."

For a moment, I heard nothing from my mTalk. Was it too late already? Had I failed before even starting? My knees weakened, and I pressed myself against the wall to keep my balance. "Dad?"

"You're not the first person called on to do something they felt unqualified to do." Dad's voice finally came over the speaker, calm and deep. "The Bible records a time when King David gave his son Solomon a huge task. A task David was unable to do himself. He asked Solomon to build God's temple. A big, important job. How do you think Solomon felt?"

I licked my lips. "Like me—a small rock floating in a huge asteroid field."

"Right," Dad said. "But David reminded Solomon about a deep and lasting truth. He said, 'Be strong and courageous and do it. Do not be afraid and do not be dismayed, for the LORD God, even my God, is with you. He will not leave you or forsake you, until all the work for the service of the house of the LORD is finished.' Gavin, God makes the promise to be with those who trust in Him. That includes you."

"But—"

"I know you don't know how to engage the reset," Dad said. "I do, but I'm not there. If we work together, we can do it. I'll talk you through the fix. I'll be the voice. You be my hands." He chuckled. "That's kind of the way God works too."

A bucket of cold water splashed in my face wouldn't have had as big an impact as that idea. (After the cold shower incident, I would know!) I stood and straightened my shoulders. "I like the sound of that."

Dad didn't waste a moment. "Good. Now, let's get started."

The next hour and a half passed in a blur. I refitted myself in my TerraSuit, strode onto the alien surface, and made the tiresome trek across the complex. Dad directed my steps to the faulty reactor—what to check on the control panel, the circuit breaker, the relays, the wiring. His voice in my ear guided every move I made, and I clung to his words.

Finally, I punched in the final code and activated the switch.

"Manual reset confirmed," KEWD said.

I smiled. "Mission accomplished!"

"Well done," Dad said. "One more thing. Before you head back to the hab-dome, take some videos of the reactors for us. The engineers will compare the readings we have on our end to actual images to check for anything we might have overlooked."

"Roger that."

It only took about fifteen more minutes to stream images of the equipment to Dad, but the intensity of my focus rivaled that of when Dad talked me through the manual reset. I didn't want to overlook any potential problem. Despite how good completing the reset felt, one heroic feat a day was plenty of action for me. "Well?" I said when I finished. "Are the reactors okay?"

"All good. Just minor damage. Those repairs can wait."

My body sagged with relief. "No other crisis?"

"Nothing we can't handle. Meteorite fragments struck a number of places on Titan's surface. Only a few impacts directly affected our livelihood. But—"

Dad hesitated.

A trickle of doubt settled in my stomach. I hate hesitations. "But what?"

"Your mom and Aurora just reestablished communication. Apparently, they were close to one of the strikes, and the radio waves interfered with their mTalks. They said one of the rover's tires got punctured. It might take them a while to make repairs."

Frowning, I turned on my heel and headed home. "How long?"

"Well—" Dad hesitated again.

Did I mention I hate hesitations?

"I'm sorry, son. There's a chance you'll have to spend the night alone in the hab-dome."

I gulped, willing myself to keep walking. "Not alone. God is with me, remember?"

"Always," Dad said. But even though I felt the smile behind his words, I felt his worry, too.

Or maybe that was just me.

||||||||| FAITH AT THE EDGE: COURAGE

Even though Gavin was afraid he couldn't manually reset the reactor on his own, he had to decide to not let his fear keep him from action. His dad reassured him that he would be right there with Gavin, talking him through every repair he needed to perform.

Knowing that he could listen to his father's voice as his

dad guided every move helped Gavin find courage to take on an overwhelming task.

The Bible teaches us that since God is with us, we can have courage too.

> Be strong and courageous and do it. Do not be afraid and do not be dismayed, for the LORD God, even my God, is with you. He will not leave you or forsake you, until all the work for the service of the house of the LORD is finished.
>
> —1 CHRONICLES 28:20

God knows we will face big challenges. He knows we will be afraid. But He wants us to understand that we don't have to face those difficult situations alone. He will not *forsake* us—which is a fancy way of saying He will not leave us. It doesn't matter if it's a big challenge, like coping with a serious illness, or a small thing, like meeting someone new or having to give a speech. Our job is to listen to God and follow His guidance. We can do that by reading the Bible and praying. This way, we can learn how to conduct ourselves in any circumstance. And there is something mighty empowering about that fact! We can have courage to act, just like Gavin did when he manually reset the power grid.

EXPLORATION ----------------------

1. Write down a time when you were quite afraid to do something—so you just didn't do that thing. Reflect on why you were afraid.

2. Recall a time when you felt prompted to act, and you did so, *even though* you were afraid. Since God is always with you, try to identify how He guided you through that situation.

3. Read Joshua 1:9. Think about a situation today where you need courage. Pray that God would guide you. Write your prayer down.

The clock had just crossed midnight. It was a new day, but I was still alone. I gulped air and willed my hands to stop shaking. The power crisis caused by the meteorite strike had been averted, but my body had yet to come down from the adrenaline rush. Thanks to Dad's help, I'd accomplished something extraordinary. And it saved the settlement.

After removing my TerraSuit, I sank into the nearest air lounger, hoping I might fall asleep. The hab-dome was running on minimal life support, so all the lights were dimmed already.

I was glad the air lounger's responsive foam didn't run on electricity. As I settled in, my muscles released their tension. But I felt the emptiness of the room. Could I survive a night alone here?

My courage misfired like an outdated HUD display, making my heartbeat surge again. Everything would be okay. Right?

I needed to hear it, so I spoke out loud. "All I need is for Mom to fix the rover's tire, Dad to organize the fleet, and everyone to come back to the hab-dome, and things will return to normal."

My voice echoed back, making the empty room seem even . . . emptier.

But what if everything wasn't okay? What if more meteorites hit? What if our supplies were damaged?

And that's when my mTalk buzzed to life. "Gavin. It's Mom. Are you there?"

Adrenaline flooded my veins again. I sprang up so fast that my lounger toppled backward. "Mom! Are you on your way back?"

Static crackled over the speaker as if Mom's mTalk was losing power. "No. Apparently, that meteorite fragment did more damage than we thought. Dad told me about your courage when you manually reset the reactor. I need you to be brave for me one more time. I don't have the tools to repair the damage to the rover, so we're stuck. And we can't stay here much longer. You've got to drive the second rover out to our location. I'll send you our position."

My mTalk pinged, pinpointing her on the map. Bile rose in my throat. "Mom, that's twenty kilometers away. You want me to drive the rover that far?"

"You can do it," she said. "You've driven the rover before."

"With *Dad*. Never on my own!"

"Maybe not, but at least you know what it feels like to sit behind the wheel. And you can use KEWD to autopilot."

"That's not the same," I argued.

"You're a fast learner. Besides, you've ridden shotgun with

Comet, helping him navigate the terrain. You probably know the area better than he does since you were the one studying the maps."

An icy chill traveled from my head to my toes, freezing me in place. "No. I can't. It's not like a VR simulation where I can reset the game if I crash. What if I get lost? Or wreck the rover? Or run out of juice? Or—"

"Gavin." Mom's voice interrupted me, soft and calm. But commanding.

I drew a sharp breath. "Yeah?"

"There is no one else. I need you." She let the words hang in the air before speaking again. "God has equipped you with knowledge, good instincts, and faith. Trust your training. But more importantly, believe in yourself. I do, or I wouldn't ask. Now buckle up. I'll see you soon."

The line went dead.

"Mom?" I said. But this time, she didn't answer.

There is no one else. Mom left me no choice. No matter the risk, I had to go. And from the sound of it, quickly. *Believe in yourself.*

Schooling my emotions, I suited up again, activated the locator on my HUD, and checked my calibrations. The airlock hatch hissed open, and I climbed into the driver's side of the rover. The front seat shifted, adjusting to my taller frame. The sudden movement unbalanced me, and I gripped the armrest.

"I can do this." I took a breath to slow the racing of my heart.

With the press of a button, the rover hummed to life. I opened the docking bay. Titan's dark world stretched in front of me like a black hole. *Lord, I believe you are with me. Help my unbelief!*

"KEWD." I pointed forward as I'd seen on an old video of a starship. "Engage rover autopilot."

My vehicle lurched out the door, guided by my grit and my prayers.

Since flat plains cover nearly two-thirds of Titan's surface, I let KEWD drive the rover at first. Autopilot worked well until Inspire disappeared from sight. But soon the rover began to bounce and rock as it rolled over a rough patch of ground. I checked the front view camera. Ridges lined the path. Perhaps a small crater? I widened the view, revealing pock marks. The rover could get me over one of those small bowl-shaped depressions. But a dozen or more? Would that throw off the position sensor in the autopilot? Or the pressure-system? If so, bad things might happen very quickly. If I continued with autopilot, I was in for a bumpy ride. I couldn't risk it.

I sighed, knowing what I had to do. "What is it with switching to manual lately?" I mumbled, pressing the buttons to take control. Maybe Comet would be impressed, seeing his younger brother drive to the rescue. Maybe Lilly would be impressed. Imagine the smile on her face! I hated to admit it, but I liked that idea even more.

"I am the Manual Master. Mr. Manual Master. *Commander* Manual Master. The CMM." I gripped the wheel and sat up straight. And immediately hit another bump, which caused me to accelerate into a donut spin. Then I overcorrected the other direction—and stalled the engine.

After taking three quick breaths, I looked through the front viewer again. If I couldn't steer that minefield better than this, I'd never get to Mom and Aurora. "The CMM suffers a setback." I fired up the rover again and let it idle. "But he is not finished. Because he's a believer. In his training. In God." I switched into gear and gritted my teeth. "And in himself."

I'd like to say it was smooth driving from there. The truth is, I might have scraped the right side of the rover against a rock, or perhaps a dozen rocks occasionally. And I might have driven about 5 kilometers per hour for twenty minutes and then 20 kilometers per hour for five minutes. And I might have taken a detour through a hilly area just so I could race to the top of a mound and back down again.

The point is, with each passing kilometer, I improved. Once I cleared the compromised area, I switched autopilot back on, confident that I could switch back to manual any time. Before I knew it, Mom's rover came into view, a spot on the horizon that grew with every passing click.

I'd made it entirely on my own.

Correction, almost entirely on my own. God was with me.

"Gavin," it was my Dad. "Did you make it to your mom and sister?"

"Roger, Dad, I have a visual on their rover now," I said.

"Praise God! Apparently their power system failed, and they were relying on their oxygen reserves and portable solar panel," Dad said.

That's why my mom hadn't called.

"Glad you've arrived," Dad said. "The good news is Max is repairing *Hopper*, so we should be ready to launch tomorrow morning."

"I'm going to try to call Mom on the radio now," I said.

My heart swelled. I'd made it to Mom and Aurora on my own, but the weight of responsibility seemed to lift knowing Dad and Comet would soon be en route.

We would be back together soon.

//////////FaITH aT THe eDGe: BeLIeVe In YOurSeLF

Gavin didn't feel qualified to drive the rover. He almost let his fear about what might happen, his fear of failing, paralyze him. He might have given up without even trying. But no matter how little belief he had in himself, he knew God would help him.

Mark 9 records a story of a man who struggled with doubt. He had gone to Jesus seeking help for his sick child. Jesus told him, "'If you can!' All things are possible for one who believes."

Instead of acting brave or pretending he had courage, the man cried out, "I believe; help my unbelief!"

And do you know what Jesus did? He honored the desire of the man's heart. Despite the man's doubt-ridden efforts, Jesus healed his child.

When demands are made of us or a challenge comes our way, anyone can feel inadequate for the task. We come up with excuses not to try. But take a lesson from the man in the story. Admit your doubts and insecurities to God. Let Him know you want to succeed, but you don't know how. Let Him know you are willing to follow His leading. Remember, God has equipped you to succeed in whatever He calls you to do.

Believe in yourself. God does.

EXPLORATION -

1. Take a survey of some of the things you do well and things you don't do well. In which situation are you most likely to seek God? Why?

2. List three projects or skills you would like to tackle but are afraid to try. Pray about each one. Set a goal to try at least one of these new things in the next week.

3. Write three "I Can" sentences. Example: I can finish my homework every day.

At breakfast the next day, Aurora pushed her Energen drink my way. "This is my thank you for rescuing us yesterday."

"Something I'll *never* tire of doing," I teased, accepting her gift. "Honestly, I'd rather travel across a meteorite field than sleep alone in the hab-dome. Even though you snore."

Aurora's eyes widened, and she swatted my shoulder. "I do not!"

Laughing, I slipped a straw into the lid. No sense saving it for later, right? I needed my energy. The Greystone family was going into mission-mode. Mom laid out our action plan last night. First, we had to assess the damage to the hab-dome and to the other modules. Then we had to make repairs. Who knew how long that would take? Still, they had to be done before focusing on expanding the settlement for the next two families, who were still scheduled to arrive by the end of the week.

I took a swallow of the heavenly fizz. "Any updates from Dad?"

"They're arriving shortly," Mom said, strolling into the room. "Fifteen minutes. Enough time for a short shower before Comet gets here to hog the hot water." She winked at me.

I got the message. Moving as fast as a booster jet, I snarfed down breakfast and rushed to wash off and change my clothes.

After KEWD had confirmed *Hopper*'s safe landing, Mom, Aurora, and I waited by the airlock. Mom paced, Aurora bounced on her toes, and I smoothed down the edges of my shirt, trying to imagine how proud Dad would be. I mean, in less than 24 hours, I had manually reset the reactor and saved the settlement, and then, with little prior training, I had driven the second rover over treacherous ground to help repair Mom's stranded vehicle. I'd proven myself. Maybe he'd put me in charge of another important project.

"Dad!" Aurora yelled when the airlock hatch hissed open. Three bounds launched her across the room and into his arms.

Helmet slung over his shoulder, Comet sidestepped the reunion and strode toward us. Mom waved, and he lifted two fingers to his forehead in greeting. "Hi, Mom. Glad you made it back in one piece—especially considering the maniac student driver behind the wheel." He shot a glance my way, but there was a slight, teasing smile on his lips.

"Mom's rover could have made it home without me, but it was *two-tired*," I quipped.

Laughing, Comet drew me into a headlock and ruffled my hair. "Good to see you too, little bro."

"Back at you." Even though I wished I could have gone with

Dad on *Hopper*, staying behind had given me a chance to stand in the spotlight without being overshadowed by Comet.

After I extracted myself from Comet's playful grip, I pulled my shoulders back and saluted Dad. "Commander, I believe you will find everything in good order here."

One arm still around Aurora, Dad pulled me into his huddle. "Praise God for His protection!"

"Welcome back." Mom accepted Dad's kiss on her cheek, then cleared her throat. "I hate to cut the celebration short, but I stayed up most of the night in the DataNode lab running diagnostics on all the systems and structures. With the approaching deadlines, we've really got to get to work."

Dad rubbed his face. "So no chance of squeezing in a quick nap? Dr. Helios had already filled our *Provider* quarters with gadgets, so getting rest between repairs was not easy."

Comet sighed. "And it didn't help that Mr. Evolt still thinks I exist to serve his every need."

Mom shook her head. "After reviewing the video Gavin took of the reactors yesterday, I had KEWD pull all the feeds and reports and cross-referenced them. I made a prioritized list and assigned each one to a partner team."

She flicked the screen on her mTalk, and a chart displayed on the closest vid-screen.

- Stabilize the containment field on reactor three
- Repair outer heat shield near the moderators on reactor two
- Realign and replace damaged solar panels
- Calibrate all Inspire life support systems
- Review meteorite strikes on the hab-dome and modules

Mom lowered her arm. "I'm going to work on the system calibrations. I've already completed about 27 percent of the work. I might find more problems, and I'll fix them as I go." She gave Dad a tired smile. "You can divide up the rest."

Rubbing his chin, Dad drew his eyebrows down into a V-shape. "The first three tasks are all in close proximity. Those require technical expertise and some real muscle work."

My heart lifted. After yesterday's heroics, surely I'd be paired with Dad. After all, Comet was *tired*. Well, I was too, but at least I'd slept in a comfortable bed last night. And I handled my Magnilox tools just as well as Comet. An almost electric tingle started in my fingertips and shot up to my chest. I held my breath.

"Comet and I will tackle those." He patted Comet on the shoulder before addressing me. "Gavin and Aurora, you are in charge of reviewing the meteorite strikes."

What? An air lounger couldn't have deflated as fast as I did. Comet got to go with Dad *again*?

While Comet puffed out his chest and nodded, I willed myself not to glare at him. Still, bitterness soured my stomach. I shifted, pressing my lips in a thin line. "Why Comet? Why not me?"

"Comet and I are already suited up to go." Dad roughed a hand over his face. "Plus, he's a more experienced rover driver and knows the system configuration and relay wiring system."

"You could drive," I argued. "It's my turn."

"This isn't about 'turns,' Gav." Dad said. "It's about survival. No time for arguments. We've got to go. Ready, Comet?"

"Yes, sir."

Frowning, I clenched my hands. I knew Dad was Titan Mission Commander, but in that moment, he was still my Dad, and he'd chosen Comet over me. Even though I'd proven myself capable,

Comet always got to do the fun stuff while I got left behind like some little kid.

Dad moved toward the hangar that housed the rover. "Nebula," he called over his shoulder. "What's our timetable for completion?"

"Uh, fast as possible?" Mom lifted her eyebrows.

"Roger. FAP." Dad laughed, following Comet out the door.

Once they were out of view and Mom had holed up in the DataNode Lab, Aurora sighed. "We'd better get started too."

I scoffed and took another sip of my Energen. "Like reviewing the meteorite strikes is important. What's the rush?"

Aurora studied me, her mouth pulled in a tiny pout. "Okay, I get it. You're jealous. But someone has to do this job too. It's a team effort."

"It's unfair." I stood, crunched the empty Energen with my fist, and tossed it in the recycling receptacle.

"Your attitude reminds me of Joseph's brothers in the Bible." Aurora planted her fists on her hips. "They were so jealous of him that they threw him into a pit, pretended a wild animal killed him, and sold him into slavery."

I tried to imagine Comet thrown into a pit. "Is that an option?"

"No!"

Aurora laughed, and I joined her.

"You know, sometimes I'm jealous of you." Aurora handed me a digital tablet. "Youngest person to walk on Titan. Hero of the great meteorite strike. Best spacewalker in the Greystone family."

Scrolling down the vid-screen, I let the information sink in. I never considered Aurora might feel jealous of *me*. I mean, she never acted jealous. In fact, she often seemed pretty content. "But you always celebrate with me. And encourage me. How can you do that if you're jealous?"

She rolled her eyes. "Because I've learned something important about jealousy—that it fills your heart with an ugly darkness. I don't want that darkness. I worship a God who calls me to walk in the light. Whenever jealousy tries to creep up on me, I confess my feelings to God, pray that He gives me a spirit of gratitude, count my blessings, and let it go."

"You're right." I closed my eyes. *God, please forgive me for my jealousy. I am so grateful for the blessings You have given me. Help me to be content.*

Soon the tension in my chest relaxed and my breath evened out, as if I'd released a heavy load. My head was clearer. I recognized that even though I didn't get to go with Dad, he still loved me just as much as Comet.

I also knew that one day, I'd be standing by his side, just like Comet. Hopefully with a Magnilox in my pocket.

IIIIIIFAITH AT THE EDGE: JEALOUSY

When Comet got a chance to work one-on-one with Dad again, Gavin experienced jealousy. Jealousy is often caused by the belief that someone else is getting to do things that you feel you deserve. Seeing someone get what you want can stir up feelings of anger, resentment, injustice, and hatred. Such sentiments, when left unchecked, can fester in our heart like mold on cheese. Aurora pointed out that God calls us to walk in the light. Gavin could not let jealousy rule his emotions.

Aurora also brought up the biblical character Joseph. It's true—his brothers were extremely jealous of him, and because of that, they did horrible things to him. But the story had a happy ending because even though Joseph's brothers tried to harm him, God turned Joseph's tragedy into good.

How do Christians handle jealousy? First, try to identify what's causing these feelings. Then, pray about it, and ask God to help you change your perspective. Practice gratitude for the blessings you have. And then—this is hardest of all—let it go.

> Surely vexation kills the fool, and jealousy slays the simple.
> —JOB 5:2

EXPLORATION ----------------------

1. Tell about a time you felt jealous. Try to describe how your body felt, inside and out, as you struggled with this emotion.

2. Review Aurora's action plan for dealing with jealousy. Write down the step that you think will be most difficult, and explain why.

3. Read Joseph's story, starting in Genesis 37. List three things you learned, two things that surprised you, and one action you can take.

First the good news: By the time Comet and Dad returned to Inspire, Aurora and I had not only helped Mom finish her calibrations in the DataNode lab but also triangulated every meteorite strike on the complex.

And now the bad news: We'd uncovered more damage that needed repairs. Plus, we still needed to complete construction of the settlement.

I went to bed tired but proud. Tomorrow promised to be just as grueling a day as today. Except, since I'd been so responsible, maybe this time Dad would take me with him.

When I plopped down in the kitchen for breakfast the next day, Comet was already there. He spooned one more bite of breakfast into his mouth and stood. "Hey, sleepyhead," he said between mouthfuls. "Ready for day two of 'Greystones save the world as we know it'?"

"Yep." Smiling, I set my Magnilox on the table next to me. "I'm ready for action."

Comet narrowed his eyes and opened his mouth, but before he could say anything, Dad walked in with his mTab.

"Good morning, Gavin. You did a great job yesterday. I'm proud of how responsible you were." Dad ran his fingers through his hair, pushing it off his forehead. "Your mom is in the DataNode lab checking updates to the Inspire network, to ensure all comms and systems are functional. Aurora volunteered to help her."

"What about me?" I asked.

Dad smiled. "I have a new assignment for you today."

My heart soared. What would it be? Realigning solar panels? Scanning the horizon for a new cryovolcano to explore? Lifting the rover with nothing but my bare hands?

"Sure." I leaned back, trying to look casual.

"I need you to monitor the constructo-bots while they resume building the new living quarters. It's an important task. The Waves and Evolt families arrive in four days, so we're on an extremely tight timeline."

Wait, what? This was even more boring than evaluating the meteorite strike damage across the settlement. I shook my head. "But—"

Dad clapped a hand on my shoulder. "There is no wiggle room in our schedule, and there are two things that require my immediate attention. Since I can't clone myself, I took the more complicated job. I'm making you accountable for the constructo-bots. You're in charge of keeping them running. Comet and I will be offsite finishing repairs."

No! Comet gets to go with Dad again!

"Don't worry," Dad said. "Just watch the vid-screen while the bots work and make sure they stay on schedule. You shouldn't have any trouble."

"But—" I started.

"Gavin, I'm very grateful you can take this task off my list of duties so I can focus on other things." Dad laced his fingers and stretched until his knuckles cracked. "Be on the lookout for breakdowns in the system. The constructo-bots have a large area to repair, and I'm not sure how the extra dust in the air will affect their sensors. If you spot anything out of the ordinary, pause the procedure and ask KEWD to run a diagnostic." He tapped my Magnilox. "I see you came prepared for such contingencies. Smart thinking."

Comet stepped toward Dad and handed him a helmet. "Just don't fall asleep on the job, Gavin. Being responsible means that you can take care of something on your own without our supervision. And we can trust you to do it right." He said those words like he was in charge of me, too! "Oh, and try the apple and quinoa breakfast casserole I made. It's divine."

As they walked toward the airlock, I choked back my anger. Being responsible? I'd show Comet responsibility. I'd watch those constructo-bots until their magnetic bolts rusted over!

And that's exactly what I did for one long, tedious hour. I watched the constructo-bots work. They drilled. And rotated. And welded. Then, they shifted five-tenths of a degree. Rotate. Drill. Weld. Move to the next target. Rotate. Drill. Weld. Shift five-tenths of a degree . . .

I stared at the vid-screen until I developed a burning sensation in my eyes.

Rubbing away the dryness, I sighed. What a waste of time! The bots were automated. The monitoring display hadn't changed, other than to update their progress. Twelve percent completion after an hour. At this rate, I'd die of boredom before they finished. How did Dad survive?

A sudden thought made me sit up straight. When Dad monitored the constructo-bots, he didn't stay glued to the seat the whole time. Sometimes he chatted on his mTalk, stepped out to scrub a filter, or did a round of cardio on a treadmill.

Obviously, the mission Dad assigned to me was running smoothly. I could open my mTab to play my favorite game, Hyper Flight Galactic, or I could reread the latest issue of *Cosmic Corsairs*. It would just be a short break. What could happen?

Adrenaline pumped through my veins as I entered Hyper Flight Galactic. The game required me to race through a maze of asteroids searching for clues while being chased by Space Drones run by the evil Dr. Howl. I would just play one or two levels.

Two levels later, I paused the game and checked the monitors.

All systems were still running smoothly. Seventeen percent completion. Slow progress, but still progress. Maybe the bots hit a complicated repair that took more time. Sort of like installing a program where some files take longer than others to download.

At least my time had passed quickly. "That's a great argument to go on to the next level," I said, pushing the continue play button. "You'll never catch me, Dr. Howl!" My virtual spaceship roared to life, and I careened around an especially nasty looking asteroid as a handful of drones fired plasma cannons and launched ion torpedoes my way.

Level fifty-seven offered a good stopping point. I paused the game, massaged my neck to ease the tightness, and checked the time.

What? I jolted to full alertness. Three hours had passed!

I looked up at the vid-screen. A blinking alert flashed red. My stomach twisted as I pulled up the details. Repairs had stalled at forty-three percent completion. Constructo-bot 65 was way off course, pinging two kilometers away from Inspire.

Nothing fast action couldn't fix. "KEWD, how do I recall an off-course constructo-bot?"

"Open settings in the constructo-bot," KEWD responded. "Select 'engage homing navigation.'"

I followed the directions. The rogue constructo-bot didn't change course. In fact, the bot didn't move at all.

I switched the vid-screen over to display feeds from individual bots so I could get a visual on the situation. The bot was wedged between two ice rocks, wheels spinning and power cell draining fast. It would have to be manually retrieved.

Sweat formed on my back. Rocking in place, I squeezed my hands into tight fists. The bots were my responsibility. Dad said he was counting on me, and I'd blown it. I'd blown it *big*.

My mind raced. Maybe I didn't need to say anything. The other constructo-bots could finish the job, and I'd pick the rogue up later. No one would have to know. Except we needed everyone to do their part, and the loss of a bot would seriously slow down construction of the settlement.

Could I recover the bot? No, both rovers were in use, and it was too risky to walk that far on my own. Not to mention my absence would be noticed, especially since I wouldn't be back for several hours. Which meant Mom or Dad would have to retrieve it.

Hands shaking, I triangulated each of their positions on the map and compared that to the constructo-bot's location. Dad was closest. He wouldn't be happy about the interruption, but the safety of our settlement came first.

I knew what I had to do. Swallowing hard, I lifted my mTalk and made the call. "Hi, Dad. I know you're busy, but . . . do you have a moment?"

||||||||||FAITH AT THE EDGE: RESPONSIBILITY

Gavin had an important task to perform. Even if the job felt boring to him, his dad counted on him to do the work. When Gavin got off track, allowing a game to distract him from completing his mission, he didn't take care of his portion of the work. If Gavin had committed to doing his best—had he taken some pride in his assignment—things might have turned out differently. As Gavin learned, a lack of responsibility often brings unpleasant consequences. Failure to monitor the vidscreens led to a constructo-bot going off course. Just like not completing your homework could result in a failing grade.

On the flip side, acting responsibly often brings rewards. If Gavin had monitored better, he might have finished the task without any assistance. Just like if you responsibly complete your homework and study for your tests, you'll likely earn a good grade.

God expects us to be responsible. In Christ's parable about responsibility, a man had three servants. He gave each a different amount of gold to take care of. Two of the men invested the money and made a profit. The third man set the money aside and didn't do anything with it. When the master called for an accounting, he took away the third man's gold and gave it to the servant with the most gold.

You may not have been given any money or serious resources to invest, but the Bible instructs us to be responsible in many other ways. As Christians, we are responsible to love our neighbors, study God's Word, and pray that He would give us direction. Keeping our focus on what we are called to do will keep us from getting off task.

EXPLORATION ------------------------

1. Tell about a time you failed to meet a responsibility. List things that led to the failure.

2. Tell about a time you successfully fulfilled a big responsibility. List the actions you took that led to your achievement.

3. Make a list of your daily responsibilities. Highlight one that is difficult to do. Use the strategies you identified in question two to help you succeed.

4. Read Matthew 25. What similar theme do you see in each parable? Who is rewarded and why? How can you be prepared for Jesus' return?

The overhead light flickered. Groaning, I set down my mTab and swatted the wall. It took two seconds for the glow to steady. "KEWD, check for malfunctions in sector seven."

"There is a loose wire connection in sector seven. Would you like schematics?" KEWD replied.

I let out a hiss of air and shut off my game. "Sure."

An image appeared with details on the problem. "Shall I page Commander Greystone to make repairs?"

I fished out my Magnilox. "Nah, I got this. KEWD, cut power to sector seven."

The room immediately dimmed on one side, making my chair cast a long shadow on the wall. I switched on the flashlight from my mTalk to see better. Using a flat edge, I popped the metal panel, exposing the inner guts of the electrical system. And oh, thrill, there was the cable, holding on to its coupling by a single strand of copper.

"KEWD, how do I fix it?"

"Apply either liquid electrical tape or silicone adhesive to the affected area. We are currently out of liquid electrical tape."

Silicone adhesive then. We had some around here somewhere, didn't we? In the storage room? Or the generator room? I saw some when I did Inspire's inventory, didn't I? Or was that *Provider's* inventory?

Dumping out the contents of the nearest drawer, I grunted. Where was it?

At least it wasn't a faulty bulb. If a bulb had gone out, we'd either have to scavenge one from another room in Inspire or pick one up on the next supply run to the *Provider*.

I slumped into my air lounger. *Provider*. At least there I knew where everything was located. And if I didn't, I could ask Dr. Sprucevine for help. Or Ms. Carver. Or maybe even Lilly Evolt.

An odd sadness swept over me, making the air in the room feel heavy and difficult to breathe. I missed my friends. Orbitus. Solar. Lilly. I even missed Lilly's dad, the cold, self-righteous "Mr. Evolt." How much longer until the hab-dome was fully operational? Too long. I mean, vid-chats were great, but by the time the other settlers arrived, I'd be unable to carry on a normal conversation without the help of a pause button and a screen filter!

I glared at the darkened circuitry and threw up my arms. "What else could go wrong?"

"Today, there is a five percent risk for an increase in radiation exposure. There is a ten percent risk of increased intracranial pressure, which would result in the shape of your eyes changing. There is a twenty percent chance of—"

"KEWD! Go to sleep." I'd forgotten the AI was still listening. "Sleeping. Goodbye."

But I had already heard too much. What if another meteorite hit the surface? What if my TerraSuit ripped like my ExoSuit had? Why did I want to live on Titan so badly in the first place? I had everything I needed on the *Provider*. And I was safe there. But here? The whole thing might just explode like a supernova.

Stomach churning, I let my Magnilox drop from my hand. It made a *thunk* as it hit the floor.

"What dropped?" Mom stuck her head into the room. "And why is it so dark in here?"

Heat rose to my face. "Sorry. It's just my Magnilox. I was trying to fix a wire, but I can't find the silicone adhesive."

"Don't you carry some in your emergency kit?"

"Oh, yeah." I gave a quick nod. "I forgot."

Mom stepped fully into the room. "Forgot? That doesn't sound like you. Unless monitoring the constructo-bots is involved." She smiled so I knew she was teasing me.

"Right." I forced a shaky laugh, then stood and dropped backward into a nearby air lounger.

Frowning, Mom cocked her head. "Is something wrong?"

I gulped. How do moms always read your mind?

"It's just—" I poked my finger into the air lounge and watched the foam adjust to my intrusion. "It's a lot of pressure living here. What if something massively horrible happens and no one from the *Provider* can rescue us on time? Or what if we can't tap into the water supply? Or I can't find the dumb silicone adhesive I need to repair this dumb wire?"

Mom pulled a tube out from the metal cubicle on the wall and bent over the open panel. "There is always danger in life. The only guarantee we have is that God is with us through it all." She tapped the wire and checked the connection. Seemingly satisfied, she sealed the panel shut. "He says that even when we walk through the valley of death, He's with us. But the fact of the matter is, He's always with us. Even when you're playing a game on your mTab. Or waiting for your friends to land."

"Really?" My voice rose an octave. "I can't see Him. I can't talk to Him."

"But you can." Mom lowered herself to the floor next to me. "Remember seeing the vast sky littered with stars? The sun winking millions of miles away? The methane lake dotting Titan's surface? In all of God's creation, we can see His invisible qualities—His eternal power, His wisdom."

I had to concede that point. The galaxy was an amazing place. But there was a lot of emptiness too. "I wish I had someone to talk to."

"The Evolt and Waves families will be here soon. But in the meantime, remember that when you're feeling lonely, you can talk to God any time," Mom said.

"How?"

"Prayer." Mom lifted a brow. "Look, I know you pray before dinner and bedtime, but prayer is for any time you need someone to listen to you. God wants a relationship with you, and prayer is how you can communicate your feelings, your longings, your frustrations." She cupped my chin for a moment. "Your fears. In fact, God encourages you to pray continuously. That's something you can only do if He is always with you. Which He is. Sort of like KEWD, only infinitely more powerful and eternally more loving and completely more capable of taking care of you."

"You're right. I never thought of it that way." I took a big breath, held it, then slowly released it. "KEWD, turn on sector seven."

"Turning on sector seven," KEWD said.

The room lit up again, chasing away the shadows.

"That's better." Mom squeezed my hand. "But think about what I said. Would you like to pray now?"

"Yes." A sudden urge to lay out everything before God dropped me to my knees. "Let's pray."

"Praying now." KEWD said. "Our Father, who art in Heaven—"

"KEWD! Go to sleep!" Mom and I snapped together.

"Sleeping. Goodbye."

I burst out laughing. Mom joined in too. Then we bowed our heads and asked God to provide us wisdom and protection and courage . . . and a few spare light bulbs. Just in case.

||||||||FAITH AT THE EDGE: PRAYER

When Gavin was on *Provider*, he felt safe. Secure. He knew where supplies were located, and he had a comfortable relationship with the staff on board. In contrast, the recent meteorite strike on Titan left Gavin feeling unsafe. Plus, he wasn't as familiar with the layout of Inspire, and he missed his friends.

All those factors made Gavin feel lonely. But Gavin's mom pointed out that he wasn't alone. God is always with him, and he could communicate with Him through prayer.

We can do the same thing. Prayer helps us connect with God and get to know Him better. We can ask God for guidance, help, healing, or strength. We can thank God for answering a prayer or for blessing our lives. Remember that though God always answers our prayers, His answer isn't always yes. But God is always there, always listens, and always cares. We can tell Him what we've done wrong and ask for forgiveness. God loves us and wants a relationship that develops when we take time out of our busy lives to talk to Him through prayer. So set yourself a goal. Find a quiet spot in your home where you can focus on God.

> Do not be anxious about anything, but in everything by prayer and supplication with thanksgiving let your requests be made known to God.
> —PHILIPPIANS 4:6

EXPLORATION ----------------------

1. The Bible has many Scriptures on prayer. Look up the following verses and write a five-word (or less!) summary of each.
   - Psalm 5:3
   - Philippians 4:6
   - Romans 12:12
   - 1 Thessalonians 5:17-19
   - 1 Timothy 2:1-2

2. Write a prayer request. Pray about it this week. Look for God to answer. When He does, record the answer.

"**G**ood morning, Mom." I scanned the galley, expecting to get high-fives and to see a big *Happy Birthday, Gavin* banner flashing across the vid-screen. Except . . . "Hey, where is everyone?"

"Gone." Mom handed me an mTab. "We've got quite a day ahead of us."

Grinning, I straightened my shoulders. Quite a day, for sure! Birthdays were always full of special little surprises. Pancakes with glittering star-shaped sprinkles in them. Chocolate cake with gooey frosting. And, of course, gifts, like the newest video game, *Übel Interceptor*, loaded right to my mTab. Everyone would spoil me.

"I guess the fun starts with the mTab," I said. Mom probably programmed a dancing birthday card on it.

I glanced at the tablet, and my stomach dropped. It was a list of work for the day.

> Dad: complete maintenance on rovers, realign communications array.
> Mom: calibrate life support systems.
> Comet: complete exterior hab-dome repairs.
> Aurora: inventory medical and science labs.
> Gavin: clean bathroom and supervise constructo-bots.

There had to be a mistake. I mean, my family didn't forget my birthday, did they? I touched my name on the mTab, and it expanded into every nitty-gritty detail of what I needed to accomplish. Sterilize shower. Restock shelves. Monitor building progress.

Frowning, I cocked my head. "What is this?"

"A list of today's missions." Mom lifted her brow. "There's a lot to do to get ready for the special day."

"And by special day, you mean . . . ?" I waited for her to acknowledge my birthday, throw out the list, and celebrate like it was 2099.

"The day when the Evolt and Waves families arrive." Mom passed me an Energen drink.

Well, I did love Energen drinks. Still, I couldn't believe it. No special pancakes. No banner. And I had to scour *toilets* on my birthday? Maybe I miscalculated the calendar. "Wait, you *do* know what day it is?"

"Of course. It's three days before our new settlers dock. And I'm already behind schedule." Mom tucked a hair behind her ear, her lips pressed in a thin line. "Aw, you look worried. Are you afraid we won't finish on time? We'll just have to prioritize everything and work extra hard today. Do you want me to check in on you later?"

"No, it's—" I gulped, swallowing my disappointment. Apparently, my birthday wasn't a priority. "It's nothing." I forced a smile. "I'll get started right away."

"Good." Mom strode for the door, then paused and pointed at me. "And Gavin?"

I perked up. "Yes?"

"Don't forget to drink your breakfast." Then, she pivoted on her heel and left me in the empty room.

Slouching, I opened my Energen and tasted it. The fizz tickled my tongue. I guess that was the most excitement I'd be getting today.

Before I got started, I wanted at least *someone* to acknowledge my birthday. After all, it was the first birthday celebration on Titan. If I took the long route, I'd pass by the observation window. Comet's assignment had pinpointed that spot for repairs. He'd remember and stop everything he was doing.

With new determination, I marched his way. Soon, I saw him on a hoverstep over the top window. I waved.

His head bobbed in response, and he pressed his wrist.

My mTalk buzzed, and I smiled. Finally, someone could wish me happy birthday. I swiped the screen and got a closeup view of his helmet. "Hi, Comet!"

"Hey, I'm kinda busy here." His voice sounded impatient. "Could you dim the lights in that room you're in. It's interfering with my vision."

"Okay." I drew the word out. "Is there anything else you want to say?"

"Oh, yeah." He put a thumb up. "How could I forget?"

My pulse picked up, waiting for the words.

"Could you restock the wipes when you clean the bathroom?" he said.

All the air went out of me. He had forgotten too. "Sure." I snapped off the lights and left, changing direction to pass the MedBay. Aurora was the best sister ever. Surely she'd remember!

When I got there, a giggle froze me in place. I poked my head into the medical lab.

Aurora stood next to a pile of containers. Her eyes were wide, and her hands were behind her back.

"What's so funny?" I asked.

Hesitating, she pulled her arms forward and switched off her mTalk. "I'm sorting medicine."

"Need any help?" I offered.

"Oh no, I'm good." Aurora grinned. "I'm only trying to get ready for the special event."

I leaned against the doorframe and crossed my arms. "Speaking of special events, do you know what today is?"

"How could I forget?" Turning her back to me, Aurora shuffled the supplies on the counter. "It's your day to clean the bathrooms. And don't forget to clean the toilet seat this time. Now get going!"

"Right." I stood there, giving her a chance to redeem herself. But she seemed totally absorbed in her work. Scowling, I took off. She'd forgotten too! Maybe Dad would remember. If he hadn't gone off site yet, he'd be in the garage fixing the rovers. I headed that direction.

"Knock, knock." I rapped on the metal wall. The sound echoed in the room. Both rovers stood at the ready, but Dad was nowhere in sight. "Hello?"

The silence stretched.

Great! He wasn't there. I kicked the nearest tread. A sharp pain shot up my leg. Some kind of birthday this was turning out to be.

No one remembered me. No one cared. I wasn't even as important as the toilet bowls.

Now I didn't even have an excuse not to get to work. But not on the bathroom. I'd wait until my bladder was ready to explode before I undertook that task. Besides, after my last failure monitoring the constructo-bots, I'd better check on them first.

I rounded the corner and ducked into the control room. Lowering myself into an air lounge, I checked the vid-screens tracking the building progress. All monitors showed green lights. "KEWD, what's the status?"

"All systems are functioning at 100 percent capacity."

Slouching, I closed my eyes. I might as well waste away in the room by myself.

My rest was short-lived. My mTalk buzzed. Opening one eye, I checked the call. Comet. "What?" I said.

"I thought I told you to restock the wipes in the bathroom."

"You did."

"But you haven't done it yet. I need you here. Now!"

As if my birthday didn't already stink! Clenching my fists, I stalked to the supply room, grabbed a container of wipes, and stormed down the hall past the galley. The lights must have really been an issue for Comet, because they were off there too. I'd show him!

"KEWD, turn on the lights."

The galley flooded with brightness. Something jumped out at me. "SURPRISE!"

Heart pounding, I dropped the wipes.

Everyone was there. Mom. Dad. Comet. Aurora. The vid-screen even showed *Provider*'s crew, including the faces of the Evolt and Waves families. They started singing, some loud and off-key.

"Happy birthday to you! Happy birthday to you! Happy birthday, dear Gavin. Happy birthday to you."

A cake frosted to look like space with planets and a rocket on top sat on the table surrounded by what I assumed were gifts tucked into empty medical supply boxes. They remembered! Everyone remembered! Joy bubbled up from my belly, and I laughed. "Wow! All this for me?"

Mom stepped forward and slipped an arm around me. "We wanted to surprise you."

Aurora bounced on her toes in front of me. "After all, it's the first birthday celebration on Titan. Another record."

"And that makes it extra special." Dad clapped a hand on my back.

"So you don't need wipes after all?" I gaped at Comet. "Not even to wipe the smirk off your face?"

"It was all a trick to get you into the room at the right time. Totally worth it to record your reaction." He imitated what I assumed to be my shocked expression, then laughed. "Want to watch the playback? It's definitely media promotion material for ASN."

"Maybe later." I absorbed all the joy and energy in the room. "Right now, I want a slice of cake with the best—" my grin grew even wider "and sneakiest—people in the galaxy."

‖‖‖‖FAITH AT THE EDGE: JOY

When Gavin thought everyone had forgotten his birthday, his mood noticeably soured. His attitude, motivation, and energy diminished. For most people, feelings of extreme pleasure and happiness accompany celebrations. The vacuum created in Gavin's day by what he thought was an oversight simply drained him. However, once he reconnected with family and friends, the bounce came back into his step.

Joy works that way. When you're happy, your body releases a chemical called dopamine that affects everything from your blood flow to your breathing. It brightens your outlook, lifts your spirit, warms your heart, and boosts your energy.

The apostle Paul had a lot of hard things happen to him. He was in three shipwrecks, he was thrown into prison multiple times, and he was almost stoned to death for declaring Jesus to be the Son of God (2 Corinthians 11:24-28). Yet in every one of the books of the New Testament that he wrote, he encourages believers to rejoice and praise God.

Joy is a frequent theme of Scripture. In Philippians 4:4, we are encouraged to always rejoice in the Lord. In 1 Peter 1:8, the apostle Peter reminds us that even though we have not seen God, when we believe in Him, we are filled with an "inexpressible and glorious joy" (NIV). Romans 15:13 encourages us to be filled with all joy and peace as we trust in God. And when that happens, we'll overflow with hope too. No matter what your circumstances, if you look for joy, you can find it in any situation.

> Count it all joy, my brothers, when you meet trials of various kinds, for you know that the testing of your faith produces steadfastness. And let steadfastness have its full effect, that you may be perfect and complete, lacking in nothing.
> —JAMES 1:2-4

Best of all, did you know God celebrates with us? Jesus once told a story about a man finding a lost sheep and rejoicing over it. He compared it to how heaven rejoices when Jesus finds us and we turn to follow Him.

So how about your day? Got joy?

EXPLORATION -----------------------

1. Write about three celebrations that made you feel joyful. Pray and thank God for each one.

2. Name two people who bring you joy. Write them thank-you notes and deliver them this week. Then plan one way you can spread joy to someone you know.

3. Read 2 Corinthians 11:24-27. List the sufferings that Paul experienced. Now read Philippians 3:7-11 and Philippians 4:4-7. What is Paul's attitude toward suffering? What is something you can be joyful about and praise God for—even in your own suffering?

"The broadcast starts in one minute," KEWD said.

Mom brushed some nonexistent dirt off her shoulder and cleared her throat. "Is everybody ready?"

"Yes." Comet nodded, shifting from foot to foot.

Aurora smoothed down a stray strand of hair and her lips stretched into a broad smile. "I can't wait to see the Waves family. They'll be so proud of what we've accomplished. Plus, I'll get to see Solar."

"Yeah. Fun times." Comet stiffened. "I'm sure they'll appreciate our hard work."

I wondered if Comet shared our excitement. After all, Solar wouldn't be the only one boarding *Hopper*. Orbitus would be coming too. They didn't exactly hit if off last time they were together.

"Broadcast in three. Two. One," KEWD counted down.

Dad looked into the camera. "Hello, Earth! We're here live from Titan with good news." He lifted a finger. "We did it."

He paused as feedback from cheering sounded from *Provider*'s end of the feed. When it quieted, he continued. "Decades ago, the alliance of space agencies on Earth sent out probes and gathered information about Titan, the second-largest moon in the solar system. The more we learned about this moon, the more humanity dreamed about one day living here."

Dad paused for a moment and then continued. "ASN acted on that vision. Recruiting the best scientists and engineers, they tackled issues like how to handle Titan's extreme temperatures and how to tap into its vast underground oceans. Then my family and I, we—" and here Dad stepped back so we could wave at the camera, then repositioned himself in front. "We were the first humans to colonize it. We explored her methane shores, and set up a sampling station. And folks, it is an awe-inspiring view from down here."

More cheering erupted, and Dad nodded. "And now, thanks to your support and prayers, we've weathered a storm that could have destroyed all of our gains. With the hopes of thousands of people on our shoulders, our family repaired the damage the meteorites did to the Inspire and to our rovers. We've completed our supply inventory, calibrated the equipment, and synchronized our systems. We set up a communication array and established a stable connection with Earth. We held our first broadcast—" he winked at me, as if to remind me about all the unexpected talking I had to do that day "—and then?" He spread his arms.

"Then we expanded the hab-dome to include space for two more families. In short, we persevered. Because of that, who knows? Maybe someday I'll be shaking your hand and welcoming you into the settlement."

On cue, he stepped away from the camera and marched toward the computer center. We followed close behind as he'd instructed us to do, circling him when he stopped.

Dad pointed, letting the camera focus on a panel on the computer console. "This is the switch that will activate the life support for the new section of the hab-dome. I would like my son Gavin to have the honor of flipping it."

What? No one mentioned this to me! The blood drained from my face as the robotic lens whirred my way. "Uh," I said, the only (not) intelligent thing I could think of to say at the moment.

Comet pushed my shoulder and laughed, as if he were in on the surprise. Aurora beamed so big I thought she might burst like a balloon—a sure indication she'd kept the secret from me too. And Mom just cocked her head with a slight smile, as if enjoying my shock.

"As you know, living in space can be hazardous. Everyone has to work together as a team and use every talent God has gifted him or her with to survive. Despite being the youngest member of our crew, Gavin lived up to this expectation after an unexpected meteor shower. Without Gavin, there would be no settlement."

He shifted his position, exposing me to the full vision of the audience. I steeled myself, fighting the urge to slap a helmet over my face to avoid all the attention.

Dad didn't seem to notice as he continued. "You see, my eldest son, Comet, and I were offsite and unable to render aid when one of our reactors was struck. Without quick action,

ASN's vision for a settlement may have perished right there, along with my wife and daughter, who were stranded on the surface in freezing conditions. Gavin executed a manual reset of the reactor—a feat that's dangerous under normal circumstances, much more during what we faced on that day. He reset the system, which preserved the equipment from radiation and exposure and saved our home. And then—" Dad's voice quavered. He reached out for Mom's hand. Grasping it, he pulled her to him and kissed the top of her head. "And then he suited up again and drove a rover solo for the first time across compromised territory. He persevered and, in so doing, saved the love of my life—" he pulled Aurora into his embrace too "—as well as his sister, my beloved daughter."

I stared at my family. Until Dad laid it out there like that, I never appreciated how close we had come to losing each other. The reality froze me in place.

Then Comet started clapping, which broke the spell. A thundering roar soon came over the sound system as we received audio of the viewership bursting into applause.

Pulling my shoulders back, I stepped toward the switch. The moment was so overwhelming, I had to thank God. How could I take full credit when He was with me the whole time, lending me courage and strength to do what needed to be done? I couldn't. I paused to bow my head.

When I finished, I lifted my chin and took a big breath. "Ready?" I asked.

"Ready!" my family (and the world) echoed.

I flipped the switch.

Light flooded the room. The system hummed to life. And with it—a new beginning.

||||||||||FAITH AT THE EDGE: PERSEVERANCE

Gavin was shocked when his dad asked him to flip the switch and activate the life support for the new section of the hab-dome. He didn't recognize how much of a difference his work had made in the survival of the settlement. After all, he'd thought, everyone had pitched in. It was through their perseverance that the family survived. And he was a major contributor to that survival.

Perseverance is a life principle that benefits all who practice it. It's a word usually associated with a challenge. Athletes need perseverance to stay disciplined and trained. Students need perseverance to study and complete demanding mental tasks. And Christians need perseverance to follow Christ when they face temptations or trials. In fact, without perseverance—the ability to stick to a task, goal, or mission—few people would succeed in life.

The Bible tells us that perseverance builds character, and this leads to hope. This idea is repeated throughout Scripture as we see many stories about people who persevere. When the apostle Paul faced oppression, he said, "I press on toward the goal for the prize of the upward call of God in Christ Jesus" (Philippians 3:14). The author of Hebrews encouraged believers to fix their eyes on Jesus as they endured suffering (Hebrews 12:1-2). Even Jesus practiced perseverance, never wavering from death on the cross.

The next time trouble comes your way, remember it takes faith and courage to overcome it. Pray that you can persevere, then dig in and do the right thing.

EDGE OF THE GALAXY

> Not only that, but we rejoice in our sufferings, knowing that suffering produces endurance, and endurance produces character, and character produces hope, and hope does not put us to shame, because God's love has been poured into our hearts through the Holy Spirit who has been given to us.
>
> **—ROMANS 5:3-5**

EXPLORATION ------------------------

1. Write down one situation where you faced a challenge that seemed impossible to overcome. Did you give up or stick with it? Why did you choose the path you took?

2. Consider Romans 5:3-5. Why do you think that perseverance builds character and leads to hope? Now read Philippians 3:14. What does it say brings hope to Paul and convinces him to persevere?

3. Name a situation where you can practice perseverance. What steps will you take to meet your goal?

"Oh! I'm so excited! They're almost here." Aurora bounced on her toes, and her words came out as fast as a laser beam. "What's their ETA now?"

"Gee, let's see." Comet folded his arms across his chest and glared up at the clock. "The Waves family is five minutes closer to landing than when you asked five minutes ago."

"Yes!" A broad smile split Aurora's face. "And how about now?"

"Ten seconds closer." Comet rolled his eyes. "I don't see why you're so excited about them joining us. It's not like they did anything to help get the place ready. I mean *we* set up their section of the hab-dome, *we* did the supply inventory, *we* repaired all the damage done to the structure, and *we* calibrated all the systems. *We* did all the work. What did they do?"

"They were training," I said. "Just like we did. But we had a head start."

"Whatever." Comet slouched deeper into the seat. "When they get here, you can kiss our quiet family breakfasts goodbye. And I'm sure Orbitus will be blasting his music."

"I like a little pep in my morning," Aurora said.

"Oh, please." Comet raised a hand. "With Solar around, it will be so peppy you won't get a word in edgewise. And she'll probably hog the hot water, too."

I leaned forward. "It wouldn't be the first time someone did that."

If Comet remembered that he was guilty of the same crime, he didn't indicate it. In fact, he kept right on ranting. "And then there's the *Mr. and Mrs.* looking down their noses at everything we do. I can just hear them now." He made air quotes with his fingers. "'Oh, Comet, you're not doing it right. Step aside and watch a pro. *This* is how you align an antenna. *This* is how you record the data. This is how you pick your nose.'"

"That never happened," Aurora countered.

I stifled a laugh, and Comet glared at me. "You think it's funny." He pressed his lips into a line. "It's not. This is an invasion."

Aurora lowered her gaze and pulled on the end of her sleeve. "Oh, please, Comet. We're growing our settlement. And some of us are really looking forward to having someone else to talk to. Someone who can share the work, too."

"Don't count on that," Comet said. "I bet we'll find out that we were better off without them."

With Comet nursing a sour expression and Aurora rocking on

her toes and shooting glances out the window, an uncomfortable silence filled the room.

I understood how each of them felt—and why. Comet saw the new people as competition, and that brought out his guard-dog persona. Aurora viewed the arrival like a slumber party, and that sent her bubbling over with enthusiasm. But had they both forgotten the big picture? Colonizing Titan and molding it into a home for humanity had always been part of ASN's plan. *And didn't Comet also believe this was all part of God's plan?*

Last week, I had read in Proverbs that "iron sharpens iron, and one man sharpens another." I wondered if the new families coming to Titan would do something similar. I could see Orbitus push-ing Comet to be a better version of himself. They'd motivate each other to work harder. And Aurora's interactions with Solar would give my sister a chance to practice some of her best qualities—kindness and compassion.

"Comet, you're wrong." I squared my shoulders. "We might be able to survive without them. But we'll never thrive. Without more families, Titan's settlement will never succeed. We need them. And they need us."

"They need us more." Red-faced, Comet pushed away from his seat. "I'm going to check on Mom."

"She said she could handle comms," I said. "Our job is to greet the Waves family."

"Well, now that's *your* job." Comet stormed off, the echo of his footsteps in sync with the pulsing of the final seconds on the clock.

Eyes wide, Aurora turned to me. "I better go after him." She swallowed. "I don't know what's gotten into him, but I think he'll listen to reason."

"Yeah, maybe if it's coming from you." I smiled, trying to look encouraging.

"Thanks." She grabbed my hand and squeezed it. "Are you okay doing this alone?"

I nodded. "I got this."

"Say hi to Solar for me." Aurora blew me a kiss and jogged after Comet.

My mTalk buzzed. "*Hopper* has landed," Mom said. "Help the Waves family load their supplies onto the cart and then get them through the airlock and to their cabins. I'll join you once your dad and I have completed the postflight checklist. Remember, the Bible tells us to welcome one another as Christ has welcomed you."

Her words hit me. I remember how it felt when I became a Christian. It's kind of hard to explain—I was both energized and peaceful, overwhelmed and untroubled, dangerous and safe, uplifted and humbled. At home and eternally grateful. And I was supposed to welcome the Waves family in the same way.

"Roger that." *God, please change Comet's attitude,* I prayed. *And help me show your love to this family you brought into our lives.*

I exited Inspire and approached the landing zone where the dust was still settling around *Hopper*.

The ramp on *Hopper* lowered. Solar and Orbitus bounded outward and across the yellowish surface. A moment later, Mr. and Mrs. Waves marched out from the ship. I stood up straight and extended a hand. "Welcome to Inspire," I said through my comms.

Eyebrows drawn in a low V-shape, Mr. Waves grunted in response. But Mrs. Waves clasped my hand and shook it.

Orbitus and Solar were still bounding across the Titan surface, showing pure joy at being some of the first kids, or people for that matter, to be on the moon. I recalled Orbitus's argument with Comet back on *Provider*, but I pressed it out of my mind as I suddenly understood what it might feel like to be in his shoes.

I turned back to Mr. and Mrs. Waves. "Hope you had a great trip. I'm really glad you're here." I pushed the cart up the ramp into *Hopper* and began loading luggage. A second later, Mr. Waves and Orbitus were there assisting as well.

A few minutes later we were in Airlock 1 and waiting to be cleared to enter hab-dome.

"We've been working hard to get everything ready for you. Had a few bumps on the way, but I think you'll be happy with your new accommodations—"

"Where are the rest of the Greystones?" Mr. Waves interrupted.

"They're working behind the scenes to make sure your first day runs smoothly."

Mrs. Waves raised her eyebrows and nodded.

"In the meantime, let me show you around." I paused, letting them cluster around me. "The layout might feel alien and empty at first, but KEWD just sent a map of Inspire to your mTalks, so once you get used to it, you won't feel so lost. Oh, and Solar . . . Aurora wanted me to say *hello*. She would have been here herself, but you know how unpredictable things are in space."

Mr. Waves snorted. "You got that right."

"Why, just the other day, as we sat down for dinner," Mrs. Waves said, placing her hand on my arm, "one of Dr. Helios's wild science experiments shut down all the electricity in the galley. Our food was cold by the time the lights came back on. Can you believe it?"

I grinned. "Sounds rough. After we drop off your supplies, how do you feel about having a snack? There's some cake left over from my birthday."

Solar pushed her way to my side. Like Aurora, she seemed ready to pop at the seams. "I'd love a slice!"

"I want a tour of the grounds first," Mr. Waves said. "I'd like to get my bearings."

I began leading the Waves family through the complex, answering questions, and trying to keep things light with explanations and a few jokes. After five minutes or so, Mr. Waves seemed to relax. He actually smiled a few times! Mrs. Waves warmed up, sharing another story about her adventures on the *Provider*. Then Solar's mTalk buzzed, and she carried on an animated conversation with Aurora while we explored the corridors. Orbitus gave me a fist bump when I opened the door to our high-tech exercise room.

By the time we reached the galley, my family was waiting for us. Solar and Aurora squealed, rushing together for a big hug.

Aurora beamed from ear to ear. "I heard someone wanted cake! I convinced Mom to make some whipped cream to top it with too!"

"Oh, Nebula. That was very kind of you," Mrs. Waves said. "And I just have to say, I appreciate all the kindness and hospitality your son has shown us. I was so nervous about today, and Gavin—"

"Gavin made us feel welcomed." Mr. Waves clapped me on the shoulder. "You've got a fine son here, Phoenix. I'm proud to have him as a neighbor."

Warmth rose to my cheeks. And I wasn't just doing my job—the friendship I'd offered was genuine. Sure, the meeting started out awkward. But if you give people a chance, they just might surprise you in a good way. Iron sharpening iron, you know?

"I'm really glad you're here on Titan," I said. "Where there's *space* for all of us."

Orbitus hooted. "Ha! *Space!* And I bet you're serving dessert on a satellite dish!"

We all broke out laughing. Even Comet smiled a little.

"Welcome home," I said. "Welcome home."

||||||||||FAITH AT THE EDGE: WELCOMING OTHERS

Today the Waves family joined the Greystones on Titan. While Comet described the Waves family as intruders invading their space, Gavin knew that expanding the settlement had always been part of the plan—and that Inspire needed more families for Titan's settlement to be a success. When the Waves family arrived, Gavin treated them with kindness and hospitality. This helped the Waves family feel at home, and it helped ease the transition into living together.

> Therefore welcome one another as Christ has welcomed you, for the glory of God.
>
> **—ROMANS 15:7**

As Christians, we are called to extend hospitality to the people around us. And Paul, in Romans 13:10, adds this: "Love does no wrong to a neighbor; therefore love is the fulfilling of the law." *Love does no wrong to a neighbor*. Those are pretty strong words.

Sometimes this can be a challenging task. It's not always easy to meet new people. And if they are not likable, it can be difficult to treat others with kindness. But remember, *while we were still sinners, Christ died for us*. God certainly didn't wait until we were "likable" before He set out to rescue us. That kind of love holds power. And when we start acting like neighbors, we can form bonds that last a lifetime.

EXPLORATION -----------------------

1. Look up the following verses, and write a short summary of each.
   - Leviticus 19:34
   - Galatians 6:10
   - 1 Peter 4:9

   What do these verses say about the central reason we are to be welcoming to others?

2. After reading these verses, list two people you could show hospitality to. Plan a kind deed and do it. Record how each person responded.

3. Do you find it easy or challenging to be welcoming to people? How about people who are not nice in return? When you find it challenging to love people, pray and ask God to give you the strength to share His love with them.

I was on my way to the galley to grab some breakfast when loud voices made me detour down a different corridor. What was going on?

"You heard what I said."

That muffled voice sounded like Comet.

"I heard. And I don't care, *Moneybags*."

That sounded like Orbitus. I picked up my pace.

"Take it back."

"Take what back? Calling you 'Moneybags'? Or calling you out for being a top-ranked jerk?"

This had to stop! I rounded the corner at a sprint and almost ran face first into Comet and Orbitus. They stood near the entrance to the lab—shoulders squared off, jaws clenched, eyebrows furrowed in anger. I didn't need infrared vision to see the heat between them.

Comet lunged at Orbitus, who pushed him back so hard that he almost fell.

After righting himself, Comet lowered his chin and clenched his fist, as if readying himself to land a blow.

Kicking it into high gear, I wedged myself between them. "Whoa, whoa, whoa, take it easy, guys."

Both stumbled back and glared past me. Which showed their determination, I guess, since I'm pretty tall. I extended my arms, forcing them to increase their distance from each other. "What's going on? Why are you fighting?"

"Your brother thinks he's some kind of prince just because you Greystones were the first ones here on Titan." Orbitus shot me a glance. "Even though everyone knows you bought your way here."

"Liar!" Comet snarled. "Someone needs to teach this Martian a lesson in manners."

"You were born on Mars too," Orbitus said.

"Well, I'm a Titan now! Have been for a couple weeks," Comet said. "One of the first."

Orbitus pressed forward. "There it is again, your arrogance and privilege."

Oh boy. This was a continuation of the argument that started on the *Provider*, after Orbitus made a poke at our grandparents' wealth.

Frowning, I crossed my arms across my chest. I turned to face Orbitus. "I thought we already cleared up that misunderstanding. You know our family never paid a single penny for the privilege of being on this mission. We were chosen for our training and skill set."

"You might not have paid, but your money still has power and influence."

His comment hit me in the gut. "You—" I paused, flicking my gaze to Comet. "Well, you actually have a point. As far as money goes."

"What?" Comet's face turned red. "You're siding with this loser?"

"No." I shook my head. "No, I'm trying to actually listen to what Orbitus has to say. But I'm not agreeing with him."

"But you said—" Comet cocked his head.

"I said he's right about money having power and influence. But he's wrong about us using money to get an advantage."

"Okay, now you're confusing me." Orbitus relaxed his stance.

"Orbitus, hear me out." I smiled, trying to ease the tension. "You seem to assume that our motive for coming to Titan and doing all we have done so far is for glory. And in a way, you're right. We are doing it for glory—but not ours. We do what we do for God's glory."

"Oh, ASN is *God* now?" Orbitus sneered.

"No," I said. "The God I'm talking about created this whole universe. Every quasar. Every planet. Every moon. And every creature or person we know about or haven't discovered yet. I mean, look at how complex life is. Even our best scientists, like Dr. Helios, only understand a small part of all this. And when you're out here, and you see how big the world is, and how small we are in comparison? It's—"

"Humbling." Comet's voice had lost some of its heat, but his face was still pinched.

"Well, I was going for awesome, but yeah, 'humbling' works." I put a hand on Orbitus's shoulder. His body tensed, but I didn't back off. "You can choose to believe me or not when I tell you that for our family, being on Titan is our way of serving God."

I shot Comet a look, then refocused on Orbitus. "And that means we serve you, too. As equals. As fellow explorers. As *friends*."

"Friends." Orbitus said, narrowing his eyes.

"Yep." I let my arm drop. "Regardless of our motivation, we share the same mission as you. We want to make Titan a settlement. We want people to thrive here, and we're willing to do the hard work to make it happen. One look around the complex will show you how committed we are to this project—how much sweat and blood we poured into this."

"Yeah, I see that part." Orbitus pressed his lips together and nodded. "I've gone through enough training exercises to know that it took a lot of time to set this all up." He grinned. "I guess no one in their right mind would *pay* for the right to work that hard."

"No kidding." I laughed. "Look, we're going to be on Titan for a long time—hopefully the rest of our lives. I don't know what the future holds, but I know we have to work together to make it happen. I mean, living in space is hostile enough without people adding their own hostility to it."

A meteorite strike flashed through my mind as I said this. *Hostile enough, for sure.*

Comet and Orbitus both lowered their gaze.

"So—" I paused, reaching out a hand to Orbitus. "Peace?"

After hesitating, he took it and shook. "Peace."

"Comet?" I released my grip and lifted my eyebrows.

"Peace." Comet shuffled forward and shook hands.

"Good." I stood between the two like a bridge. But it was time to get us all on the same side. "Anyone want to join me for breakfast? I don't think I can make it until—wait, what do astronauts call that midday meal?"

"Launch!"

Orbitus and Comet said the punchline at the same time. Wide-eyed, they looked at each other and then burst out laughing.

"I'm in," Orbitus said.

"Me too." Comet nodded.

"Good," I said, turning toward the galley. The two flanked me on either side.

"Okay, I got one," Orbitus said. "What kinds of songs do astronauts sing?"

"What?" I asked.

"Neptunes!" Orbitus replied.

"Oh," Comet groaned. "How about this one? Why don't astronauts hang out with celebrities? They don't want to get starstruck!"

Breakfast ended up being just the kind an astronaut would love.

A blast.

||||||||||Faith at the edge: Peacemaking

When Gavin discovered Orbitus and Comet about to get into a fistfight, he stepped in. He validated Orbitus's viewpoint, but also pointed out Orbitus's misunderstanding by describing his family's purpose on the Titan mission. Plus, Gavin reminded both boys how long their future there on Titan together would be. His quick action and friendly approach eased the tension and helped the two come to a peaceable resolution.

As Christians, we can often find ourselves at odds with the world. Perhaps we have a classmate who doesn't understand why we do certain things, like why we pray, or who outright opposes what we believe. But God instructs us to live peacefully with those around us.

> Live in harmony with one another. Do not be haughty, but associate with the lowly. Never be wise in your own sight. Repay no one evil for evil, but give thought to do what is honorable in the sight of all. If possible, so far as it depends on you, live peaceably with all.
>
> —ROMANS 12:16-18

That doesn't mean we won't have disagreements or that if we do face a conflict, we have to give in. Instead, it means that we stand firm but try to resolve our issues in a manner that won't further escalate the problem. Hopefully, our efforts will lead to a place where both parties can treat each other in a civil fashion.

Keep in mind, there is no promise that our efforts will result in peace. After all, there will likely be people in your life that simply won't be happy around you, no matter what you do. But that's where the "if possible" comes into play. If possible, make peace. If not, respectfully disagree and walk away.

EXPLORATION ----------------------

1. Think of a time when you had a conflict with someone else. How did the situation end? Why do you think it ended the way it did? What would you do differently next time? What would you do the same?

2. Check out these verses on peacemaking. Write a short summary of each.
   - Proverbs 12:20
   - Romans 14:19
   - Hebrews 12:14

What similarities do you see in these three verses?

Pick a verse to memorize. Write it below.

GLOSSARY

airlock: a small room with controlled pressure and parallel sets of doors so that astronauts can move between a pressurized area and the vacuum of space.

air lounger: a durable, inflatable sofa.

Alliance of Spacefaring Nations (ASN): a coalition of twenty countries on Earth as well as the first established nation on Mars. From its command center on Earth, the ASN's job is to organize compatible spacefaring teams, plan their missions, and deploy the groups to the various settlements and outposts around the solar system. The alliance believes in community, innovation, bravery, and hope for a better life for humankind. Part of the oath that ASN astronauts take is "To serve others by selflessly going beyond the known limits of humankind." The ASN's main competitor is Galactic Prime, a large space exploration corporation.

Astrobotany: a section of *Provider* twenty times larger than any other section and dedicated to an aquaponics greenhouse. Dr. Sue carefully operates this climate-controlled farm, raising plants, animals, and insects to provide food for the platform and the settlement. Eventually Inspire will start its own greenhouse on Titan with plants from this lab.

Beyond: the interplanetary spaceship transporting people and supplies to *Provider*. It has limited cargo space and only makes three supply runs to *Provider* each year.

Bliz-Zero Gear: a brand of winter outerwear including parkas, pants, and face masks. With proper hand and foot coverings, Bliz-Zero Gear can sustain the wearer through Titan's -290°F temperatures.

constructo-bot: the fleet of remote-controlled robots used to build new colonies and orbital platforms, collect samples for scientific study, and maintain equipment from a distance. The Greystones program, oversee, and occasionally correct the robots' operations. Each robot is identified as "CB" followed by a dash and a unique number.

Cosmic Corsairs: a popular series of e-comics set in the far-away Alpha Centauri star system.

cryovolcano: a type of volcano that expels ammonia, methane, or water vapors into an extremely cold environment that is at or below the freezing point of these compounds.

DataNode: refers to the laboratory and storage area where the data servers and systems are housed.

Deployable Underground Gadget (DUG): an autonomous probe—shaped like a torpedo—that carries an onboard nuclear reactor to power a drill through layers of ice. Sensors built into the probe guide it to a pre-programmed depth in the ice, gathering data along the way. DUG collects samples from its destination, melts the ice around itself, and then reverses course back to the top.

Electromagnetic Ytterium Equipment (EYE) mask: flexible, membrane-like mask that is placed over the viewing window of a helmet to help increase the wearer's vision in Titan's thick atmosphere. An EYE mask detects much more of the electromagnetic spectrum than visible light. It is connected with a transmitter in a space helmet to send the additional information directly to the optical nerves of a user's eyes.

ExoSuit: a type of spacesuit explorers wear in space while doing spacewalks.

Energen: a drink loaded with vitamins and calories.

Galactic Prime: a space exploration company; the chief competitor of the ASN.

hab-dome: the living area of a settlement, containing sleeping quarters, galley, lavatories, and recreation spaces. Hab-domes are usually subdivided to have separate lavatories and sleeping quarters for each family in the settlement.

hab-suit: a protective suit that the Greystones and other explorers wear while inside space stations like *Provider* or surface structures like Inspire.

Heads-Up Display (HUD): a functionality built into helmets that overlays the viewing window with a display of digital information such as navigation information, maintenance repair instructions, and learning about the surrounding environment.

Hopper: the transport ship that travels between *Provider* and Inspire. Also known as the Titan lander, *Hopper* is designed to ferry people and supplies between the orbital station and the settlement.

hoverstep: a small, drone-shaped craft that lifts people up and down so they can reach high places.

Inspire: settlement being constructed on the surface of Titan. Inspire will serve as the home to the initial settlers and later be expanded to accommodate future settlers. Inspire is powered by a solar array field and nano-fusion reactors. Inspire has multiple airlock entrances and a backup power system in case of emergencies.

ionic drill: a large drill head that spins through rock-ice while emitting a purple light.

J-Pak: thruster pack used to allow flight and maneuverability in space. A modified version will allow flight on the surface of a planet or moon.

KEWD: the Greystone family's AI (Artificial Intelligence), deployed by Nebula Greystone to serve the whole family. ASN families have their own dedicated AI that is not networked to other AIs or systems. This allows for a level of privacy and personalization. KEWD is programmed into all of the Greystones' devices and can therefore anticipate the Greystones' thoughts and needs in many locations and circumstances. It assists with a variety of tasks, such as auto-driving vehicles, solving math problems, helping with communications, providing real-time information and instructions, monitoring the condition of various systems, performing diagnostic scans on equipment, sending wake-up calls and alerts, and passing along commands to constructo-bots or other systems.

Luna: a name for Earth's moon.

Magnilox: a tool used for releasing and locking connectors.

MedBay: the medical laboratory and area at Inspire.

mining-bot: a bot used to remotely mine the surface of Titan for necessary raw materials used to construct the settlement.

mTab: a handheld device with a holographic screen that provides information to the user. The mTab devices are interconnected with the user's mTalk.

mTalk: a wrist-worn device that gives the wearer critical real-time information and allows direct communication with other mTalk wearers. The Greystones' mTalks are also loaded with KEWD to give them constant access to the advanced AI.

Nano-bionetics injector: a machine that guides an ionic drill head through Titan's icy surface while delivering a special solution to help soften or melt the ice around the tip of the drill head.

Provider: the orbital platform constructed by ASN to provide a gateway to Titan, Saturn's largest moon. This space station is crewed by seven and can accommodate an additional thirty people. The Astrobotany lab is the largest section of the platform. *Provider* is powered by its own solar array and provides residents with simulated gravity.

rover: versatile and agile vehicle used to traverse the surface of Titan. Each rover has enough room to carry six people and is equipped with its own life-support system, which is capable of supporting its six occupants for up to two weeks.

Spidey: the Greystones' nickname for the spindle-legged, remote-controlled robot that positions and launches their first DUG into a Titan cryovolcano.

StarNav: ASN's navigation system for flight control of *Hopper* and other short-distance spacecraft.

TerraSuit: a protective suit used outside of the hab-dome that the Greystones and other explorers wear while exploring and working on the freezing terrestrial surface of Titan.

Titan Observation Port (TOP): a module of *Provider* where a wide row of windows provides a view of Titan.

Titan Operations Command Module: sometimes called "TopCom," this is the section on *Provider* that the Greystones use for remote building of the Inspire settlement on Titan. The module's walls are filled with vid-screens that provide live video feeds and updates from Inspire and the constructo-bots. The Greystones operate the constructo-bots from the Commander's Station and other consoles within this module.

vid-chat: a system of communication that allows people to chat over video throughout the solar system.

vid-screen: a mounted screen with speakers for displaying videos or other content.

Virtual Reality Simulator: a simulator dedicated to flight training using a virtual reality headset to create an immersive, lifelike simulation.

walker-suit: a nickname for the ExoSuits that astronauts wear in space while doing spacewalks.

acknowledgments

Thanks to my wife, Ashley, for allowing me to continue creating stories; none of my writing would be possible without you, your encouragement, or your patience. You were my first editor long ago on my first book, *Evad*, which was the beginning of the journey.

Thanks to my kids Kinley, Elsie, Waverly, and Declan. You continue to inspire me with your ideas. My books are for you. I hope *Edge of the Galaxy* encourages you and your generation to dream big, imagine, and explore. May you follow God's leading in your hearts and minds even when it seems to go against what others believe.

Larry Weeden, you gave me practical writing advice and explained the challenging road of publishing. But you also encouraged me and gave me hope. You have continued to coach and encourage me all these years. Thank you.

Vance Fry and Mike Harrigan, thanks for your edits and ideas as *Edge of the Galaxy* was on the launch pad. Your insight and thoughts helped craft a book ready to launch on a galactic adventure.

Mom and Dad, as always, you continue to encourage me with my writing journey. Thank you for allowing me to explore my imagination and for always letting me know how much I am loved.

Steve Laube, you said I have 500 books in me. Here we go! Thank you for continuing to find the right home for each book and encouraging me not to settle but to aim high (even outer-space high) with my aspirations.

To the publishing and marketing teams at Focus on the Family and Tyndale House Publishers: Thank you for doing yet another project with me and allowing me to take my ideas and turn them into something tangible that kids and families can experience.